sir HUMPHREY of BATCH HALL

THE BATCH MAGNA CHRONICLES, VOLUME TWO

PETER MAUGHAN

This edition published in 2019 by Farrago,
an imprint of Prelude Books Ltd
13 Carrington Road, Richmond, TW10 5AA, United Kingdom

www.farragobooks.com

ISBN: 978-1-78842-126-3

Have you read them all?

Treat yourself to the whole Batch Magna Chronicles series:

The Cuckoos of Batch Magna
Welcome to Batch Magna, a place where anything might happen. And often does...

Sir Humphrey of Batch Hall
The course of true love never did run smooth – especially not when badger baiters are involved.

The Batch Magna Caper
Sparks fly as a real gun and a real crook find their way into a historical re-enactment at Batch Hall.

Clouds in a Summer Sky
The steam boat *Batch Castle* starts carrying passengers once more, leaving local taxi magnate Sidney Acton with a score to settle.

The Ghost of Artemus Strange
Sir Humphrey's plans to play Father Christmas are thrown into doubt, and ghostly goings-on turn more chaotic than planned.

Turn to the end of this book for more information about Peter Maughan, plus – on the last page – **bonus access to a short story** by the author.

Emma's book

Chapter One

Through all the bare, grey days of winter, the coming marriage of Sir Humphrey Franklin T. Strange, the 9th baronet of his line and squire of this March, and the Honourable Clementine Wroxley, eldest daughter of a Shropshire baron, had waited for the denizens of Batch Magna and its valley like the promise of summer itself.

And now, early on the morning of the day, it rained, a sudden high downpour off the mountains, crossing the border like an invasion, swept in on Welsh winds.

It fell on this valley in a place that has been called the forgotten country, where England turns into Wales and Wales back into England around the next bend. A valley lost among its twisting, high-banked lanes and ancient wooded hillsides on a road to nowhere in particular, and in no particular hurry to get there.

It fell on the small black and white farms among orchards, and the Conqueror's castle on a hill, a fortress once against border incursions and the forces of Cromwell, its loopholes blinded now with creeper, its walls open to Welsh rain and rabbits.

It fell on the Marcher village of Batch Magna, the cross of St George, hanging limply from the Steamer Inn, a riposte to the doused-looking red dragon of Wales above the door of the post office and general store. On its river and the great, immemorial yew, rusting iron bands holding in a girth spread wide with age, standing above a church which bore in its nave the marks of Norman chisels, and among its gravestones a sundial which told the time in Jerusalem.

And on the tall, star-shaped chimneys and red sand-stone-flagged roofs of its manor house, Batch Hall, home to the Strange family for over four hundred years, set with Elizabethan ornateness in what was left of its park. A striped black and white confection of half-timbers and grand gable ends that age had settled out of true, giving the whole a tipsy look, a foolishly happy, disreputable air, suggestive of a down-at-heel aristocrat, ruined but jaunty in a battered silk topper and with a bottle in his pocket.

There, in one of the bedrooms which wasn't collecting the weather in buckets, Sir Humphrey, alone in the big four-poster for the last time, as he had told himself, closing his eyes on that thought, slept blissfully on, his prized New York Yankees base-ball cap next to him on the bedside cabinet, his dreams lit with the stag-night fireworks fired from the ruined keep of Batch Castle. Fireworks which, this time, had ended with Catherine wheel hearts dazzling the midnight sky.

It had been midnight when he had first kissed the woman he was to marry today, kissed her on the banks of the River Cluny. Kissed her on the eve of returning to a fiancée waiting for him in New York – something he'd had words with himself about, several times, the next day, before going back to thinking about Clem, and then starting guiltily, as if caught doing it, and thinking about his fiancée instead, before …

Because when he'd kissed her, kissed her in the mid-night-scented darkness, under fat summer stars the colour of cider, the night had gone up.

The sky above them shook rigid with light, as more giant rockets and Big Bertha sky bombs exploded there, part of the annual fireworks display in the castle marking the end of Regatta day.

And more stars had bloomed, bursts of them, falling in coloured showers on Batch Magna and its river as, wonderingly, he'd kissed her again.

And now he had taken the memory of that night to bed with him, and had been overwhelmed again by all that had happened to him, the movie his life had turned into since a great uncle he hadn't known he'd had died in a place he'd never heard of. He had gone from a short-order cook living in a second-floor walk-up in the South Bronx to a baronet in a four-poster bed in a manor house – even if the roofs did leak.

He'd *even* got the girl – the right girl, in the end.

While Humphrey slept on, his bride-to-be, in her caravan behind the yards of the Batch Valley Chase, had been woken by the sound of rain on the roof.

She glanced anxiously at the clock on the bedside cabinet, and saw with relief that it was not yet six o'clock.

She lay back and closed her eyes again, confidently trusting her day to Batch Valley's own way with its weather and Miss Wyndham, who knew about these things.

Chapter Two

Some hours later, while his wife struggled to light the Rayburn which sulked in the kitchen of the rectory, and which only a week ago she had let go out now that it was officially summer, the Reverend Cutler was in his study, where bronchitic mice wheezed and sang behind the wainscoting and browsed the nibbled shelves of *Parish Register, Crockford's Clerical Directory* and rows of *Ecclesiastical Law*.

He was on the telephone, wearing a pained expression and mittens, knitted for him by one of his volunteers. The rector had inherited damp, over three hundred years of it in the house, and on days like this the Norman masonry in St Swithin's next door ran with it. The rector, no longer young himself, felt it in his extremities.

Once there would have been a small army of local artisans at hand to put things right, and the cellars stocked with tithes from the farms of the valley and hung with estate game, and gifts of port and Madeira. Now, in a house which cost considerably more than his stipend to run properly, he kept the coal they had to be careful with in the wine cellar, and wore his mittens when it rained.

The rector, sitting at his desk, where he'd been putting the finishing touches to his wedding address, with its stern twin themes of duty and responsibility, shifted in his chair. He had taken a call from one of his small band of parochial helpers, a woman who *always* had something to say, and who was now busy saying it, this time about the church fête, planned as part of the day's celebrations on Taddlebrook Leasow.

The Rector's mouth opened and closed again on an attempt to suggest that, given the weather, there almost certainly would not now be a fête, or, for that matter, anything else planned al fresco for the day.

His shoulders slumped despairingly, as barely without pause she moved on to the necessity of the right positioning of her white elephant stall. His head went back and he gazed up at the ceiling with a small doleful smile, a martyr to damp and patience.

And then his gaze shifted to the study window, and he blinked.

New to a part of the country which made up its own weather, and having, only an hour ago, been assured through the authority of the BBC that the rain was widespread and in for the day, it took some moments for it to sink in that out there, on a rectory lawn in Batch Magna, the rain had stopped, and the sun had come out.

And shining above it, sitting as solid as a croquet hoop in the sky, was a rainbow.

The rector put the telephone down on the voice on the other end, and walked across to the window, slowly, wonderingly, as if beckoned. He had been hoping for a sizeable contribution from the fête for the church and rectory damp-course fund, and he looked with gratitude at what he had so miraculously been given.

A Scot by birth, whose first act of his incumbency had been to remove the Popish touch of blue velvet curtains from behind the altar, and whose God still faced north on Sundays, when in his soul a grey rain fell again on granite, the rector allowed himself, for one brief, giddy moment, to believe that the God who had followed him from childhood had relented, and smiled on the church and rectory damp-course fund.

The rector abandoned himself to the idea again later, when bumping into Miss Wyndham on the way round to the church, the full peal of eight bells ringing the changes, bell on joyous bell spilling from a tower from which the Stars and Stripes shared the day with the cross of St George and the red dragon of Wales. Voicing the thought to her diffidently, and with an abrupt giggle, the sun, climbing in a blameless blue sky, warming him like an extra schooner of sherry.

Miss Wyndham, her thoughts elsewhere, looked startled.

Miss Wyndham's thoughts had been elsewhere since getting up at first light to try the mauve outfit on again, and then the royal blue, then the mauve, and then the blue again. Invited to sit in the reserved front pews with members of the two families, she had been dithering in anticipation all day.

"When it rains like that here before six in the morning, Rector," she told him with a touch of impatience, her hat, which matched the royal blue outfit she'd finally decided on, and which bore a confection of silk flowers, ostrich feathers, pressed chiffon and hat-pins, wobbling, "it *always* stops before eight. And in the summer the sun always comes out by ten. *Always!*" she insisted, on a sudden, high note of gaiety, already on her way again, quivering as she had been quivering all day at the thought of what waited ahead. Quivering and humming, and erupting now and then into loud, vague bursts of song, sudden flights of sheer pleasure.

Even Mrs Medlicott, standing outside the packed church with a group of village ladies, had to admit that Sir Humphrey had made an effort. Although it wouldn't have surprised her in the least, she made it known, had he turned up wearing his baseball cap and one of those ghastly shirts of his. Both the bridegroom and his best man, Phineas Cook, were in morning dress, with black silk toppers and yellow chamois gloves. But they all agreed that Phineas Cook looked the worse for wear, which in their experience was nothing new. He lived on the river, on one of the houseboats, and it was common knowledge what went on there.

And then a whispered discussion of some of the things that had gone on there lately was interrupted by the arrival of the bride and her father.

They had been driven to the church on the black and gold wagonette John Beecher kept in his coal yard in the village. John, who, as Joint Master with Clem of the Chase, was in his Master's pine green coat, with silk topper, had put both his pair of Welsh cobs on for the day, combed, plaited and beribboned, their coats brushed to a gloss, short legs picking up the pace smartly as they did a tour of the village first, the harness streaming with white ribbon, the sun melting in yellow pools on the polished brass.

And when Clem's father handed down his daughter, even Mrs Medlicott approved of this Clem.

The other Clem, the one usually dressed in stained riding breeches and a man's shirt, the one who rolled her own and knocked back pints of Sheepsnout cider, and arm-wrestled the men in the public bar of the Steamer Inn, when she wasn't wielding a siding knife among the gore in the back yard of the kennels, butchering dead farm stock for the hounds, that one was immediately forgotten.

This Clem carried a delicate bouquet of lilies-of-the-valley, and was wearing, it was said, the wedding gown first worn by her grandmother, in Edwardian net with ruched ruffles and flounces and a swagged skirt. The diamond tiara from that time had long been sold to help patch up the Wroxley finances, but the lace veil was the original, Clem nervously moving it from her face like hair as she made her way on her father's arm towards the open church door, where Ffion Owen, her chief bridesmaid, waited, face frozen with stifled giggles, and glancing now and then with lowered eyes at a group of village lads standing, laughing and nudging each other, along the top of the churchyard wall.

Clem's headdress was secured by a circlet of flowers, and the church was scented with more wild flowers, Ffion's mother, Annie, had seen to that. Added to those from the florist in Church Myddle, on window sills and chancel steps, and around the altar, were vases and urns of flowers from the hedgerows and fields, dog roses and honeysuckle, and flowering grasses, sedges and meadowsweet from the banks of the Cluny, with more flowers, small posies of them, tied to the pew ends, as if she had wanted to bring as much of the valley, as much as summer, in as she could carry.

The organ notes of Mendelssohn died, and Humphrey stood with Clem in the jewelled light from the east window, under a hammerbeam roof with owls and otters carved into its timbers, his family's history running through the names around them on stone, brass and marble on the lime-washed walls. And on a 17th century high tomb, where the alabaster figure of the first baronet, Sir Richard Strange, lay in plate armour with his sword and his shield of arms painted on his breast, his hounds and children gathered below him, and his Welsh wife Hawis by his side.

"Wilt thou," the Reverend Cutler addressed him, "have this woman to thy wedded wife …?"

Humphrey grinned and shifted his large frame. "You *betcha*!" he couldn't wait to get out, grinning it at Clem.

The rector looked pained.

"Sir Humphrey …?" he prompted.

"Humph," Humphrey said automatically.

And then, realising, "Sorry! I do, sir. I do. *You betcha I do!*"

And the bells that rang out for Sir Richard and Lady Hawis rang out for Humphrey and his bride, rang from hillside to hillside, as the couple stepped out of the ancient dimness into sunlight and a shower of confetti and rice.

Chapter Three

The church fête was not all that was al fresco after a champagne reception in the Hall.

The celebrations, organised by the Regatta committee, which did this sort of thing every year, were held on Taddlebrook Leasow, a long stretch of pasture running down to the Cluny, the property until last year of the estate and donated for the day by the new owner as a wedding present.

And it seemed that the entire valley and beyond, both sides of the border, had turned up for them.

Under red, white and blue bunting and the flags of three countries, something like a small county show had sprung up.

There was a dog and a goat show, ferret racing, a tug-of-war, bale-tossing and log-splitting, and nail-hammering competitions – the latter won with ease by John Beecher, driving with a single blow a six-nail as straight as a bullet into solid oak. A falconer with an amber-eyed golden eagle lifting its wings in a river breeze, a juggler, a fire eater, and an escapologist, chained and padlocked in a sack suspended from the back of a truck. And to bells and tambourines, an all-girl troupe of Morris Dancers, in Lincoln-green silk shorts and singlets, watched by a largely male audience with a sudden and thoughtful interest in folk dancing.

And later a trad jazz band, The Church Myddle Stompers, warmed up on a large grain trailer under more flags and bunting. And when the newlyweds, dressed for the train afterwards and a fortnight's honeymoon in London, stopped in front of them to receive more best wishes, and to have another photograph taken for a village family album, the band, for want of a more appropriate number, broke into 'Ain't She Sweet', the vocalist belting it out, while Humphrey, who couldn't have agreed more, grinned and held her to him in a beefy grip.

The couple had a ride each, once round the field on a pony and trap for a pound, lost two more pounds betting on Owain Owen's hob ferret, rolled pennies, played skittles, shot arrows, and threw hoops, coconuts and darts, and following an invitation to get into practice for married life, plates, a pound's worth each at the crockery-smash stall.

And while Clem dutifully stopped at the WI's stand, under a sign 'New Things To Do With Fruit', Humphrey watched a sword swallower, standing avidly among a small group of village children, their mouths open between licks at the jumbo ice-creams he'd treated them, and himself, to.

After putting in an appearance at the beer tent, where more champagne was waiting on ice, Humphrey paused alertly, his nose picking up another smell on the air, mixed with that of beef burgers and hot-dog onions from the food stalls. Roast lamb, he identified. A whole lamb, skewered and turning on a spit above a bed of coals on the other side of the ground.

Clem firmly steered him in another direction, towards another tent.

Jasmine Roberts, who lived on the *Cluny Queen*, one of the four houseboats on the river, was a psychic, a 'World Famous' one, according to the sign at the entrance to her bell-tent, with 'A Special Rate for Pets'.

Clem had an appointment.

Jasmine, her hair with a shine to it like coal falling almost down to her waist, was sitting in front of a fold-up table, dressed for work in a voluminous green silk dress printed with golden sun faces and zodiac circles, and wearing her crescent-and-hand necklace and Egyptian charm bracelets, her plump hands heavy with fish and abraxas rings.

She smiled up at them when they came in as if through tears, and sniffed, a happy memory of the wedding service throughout which Jasmine had wept quietly and steadily.

Clem took the chair on the other side of the table and Humphrey stood solemnly next to her, large hands clasped in front of him.

Jasmine asked for Clem's plain gold wedding ring, and holding it to her, her breasts filling the green silk like pillows as she leaned forward over it, she closed her eyes on their future.

"*Ahhh*," she breathed then, smiling indulgently at what she saw there. "There's nice! A family in the Hall again, warming its old stone and timbers ..."

She looked up at Humphrey.

"You'll need to put in a couple more bathrooms, Sir Humphrey," she said cheerfully.

"Humph," Humphrey said automatically.

Clem looked aghast. "All girls?"

Jasmine closed her eyes again.

"No ... No, not all girls – there's boys there as well."

"How many?" Clem asked, her voice going up a couple of registers.

Jasmine frowned. "Hard to tell, darling, really ... They won't stay still long enough, see. They're all over the place, like ferrets. Up and down the staircase, in and out of rooms and the outhouses, down on the river. Everywhere they are. Like my lot. Still," she added reassuringly, "perhaps some of them are friends, like, from the village."

Clem looked up at her husband and smiled weakly.

Humphrey was rubbing his hands, his expression making it clear that, no matter what the future number of their children might be, he for one couldn't *wait* to get started on them.

He would have liked to have kept his present to Clem a surprise, but that had hardly been possible.

Erected on Taddlebrook during the morning, when she had been otherwise engaged, it was now the highest structure in Batch Magna, topping both the church tower and the Hall's chimneys.

Humphrey had hired the big wheel for the day from the funfair which turned up annually for the Regatta. It stood on the same spot at the river end of the ground as it had last year, when he and Clem had ridden on it as near strangers, on the eve of his return to New York and what he had thought was his future.

He put an arm around her now, as he had then – she had made sure of that, Big Clem, who was always among the first in the field to put her mount at the riskiest hedges, and who, for a bet one winter during repair work to St Swithin's tower, had skimmed up the outside of the scaffolding in the dark to the top, clinging to him and screaming with fright like a teenager.

The wheel rushed the sunlit air, showing them for that brief moment the blooming valley spread before them, as it had done unseen in the darkness that night, the reflected light then on the river glimmering below them at its heart like something buried and shining there.

Chapter Four

A week later, Commander Cunningham and the First Lieutenant, as he referred to Priny, his wife, were enjoying one of those jollies that sort of *happened* on the river, starting with somebody visiting for whatever reason from another houseboat, and somehow managing to end with most if not all of the rest of the river following in turn up the gangway.

This particular jolly was happening on the deck of their houseboat, the *Batch Castle,* one of four Victorian paddle steamers now permanently moored at Batch Magna. Houseboats which, apart from the *Castle,* belonged to the estate still, and which, up until the last war, along with a fifth paddler, had made up the Cluny Steamboat Company, carrying passengers, goods and livestock as far upriver as Shrewsbury and back.

The old CSC ticket office, and the landing stage with its Victorian lamppost that had once flared in the river mists, were now part of the *Castle's* moorings, the office used as a storeroom and a spare bedroom when friends and family came to stay, and the fire was lit again in the waiting room. There was a wooden triangular pediment still under its eaves, like that of an old branch line station, scented yellow and crimson rambling roses on the walls, and hanging baskets of geraniums and petunias, and begonias blooming in the fire-buckets.

The fifth vessel from that time, the *PS Sabrina*, the old Roman name for the River Severn, came to grief not long into service when her boiler blew, quite spectacularly, during a river race. Her remains lay upriver now, a wreck used as a diving board for generations of village children, her broken wheels a nesting place each year for moorhens.

The four other paddles had been converted to houseboats in the late Forties to cater for the duck-shooting parties that hardly ever came, and then for holidaymakers who did so in even fewer numbers, and afterwards were used variously as storage and hay sheds, and accommodation for estate workers, until today and their present tenants.

While Priny sat with Annie Owen and Jasmine Roberts on a sun-lounger with a fringed top, part of a patio set meant to grace the back garden of a suburban semi, and bought on weekly payments from one of Bryony Owen's catalogues, her husband was entertaining two landlubbers who had also managed to end up there; Shelly, Humphrey's widowed mother, replanted from the Bronx, and now unofficial housekeeper at the Hall, and Miss Wyndham.

Shelly was still thanking her doodle-brained son's lucky stars for Clem and his rescue from the clutches of the Piranha, as she'd almost immediately named his, happily, ex-fiancée on first meeting her. Anybody else, as long as his name wasn't Humphrey, would have seen her coming a mile off. Yeah, sure, she'd said, what the Piranha had in mind for the Hall and what was left of his estate, *was* different from his usual, nutty, get-rich-quick schemes – it was a get-taken-to-the-cleaners-by-the-Piranha-scheme. Her son, who had often boasted idly in the past of being a hotshot, a mover and shaker, now found that he was one, according to the Piranha, and had taken to wearing red Wall Street suspenders and talking about margin awareness, and profit curve indicators and fenced dollar allotments. Shelly could have hit him.

And then he'd met another girl, and kissed her, down by the Cluny.

The Commander was sitting with the two women at the round white plastic deck table in the shade of a large floral parasol, part of the same patio set. At his feet, Stringbag, the Cunninghams' young black and white Welsh collie, dozed contentedly.

Shelly, who'd dropped in on her way to the shop to see if there was anything the Cunninghams wanted, and was still there nearly two hours later, was talking about the trip on a Thames pleasure cruiser her son and Clem had made yesterday.

Humphrey had phoned last night and told her about it. The Thames was a fine, big river, Mom, he'd said, like the Hudson and Mississippi, which was all very well, but give him the Cluny any day. In fact, Humphrey had reckoned, there was *no* river like the little ole Cluny.

"Well …!" Miss Wyndham said, and looked both pleased and quite tearful for a moment as she glanced over at the river, proud as a parent.

The Commander nodded his approval. He liked that, a man going into bat for his river. And Humphrey, of course, had been spot on. There *was* no river like the Cluny. Or if there was, then the Commander hadn't come across it. Nor no valley quite like this one.

And on such a day, the smell of the river freshened after rain again earlier, the washed sky above the small valley a watercolour blue, a storybook sky with a few white, blossom-fresh clouds dabbed here and there on it, the air sweetened and with a polish to it of a young apple.

Downstream, calling from the moorings of the Owens' boat, the *Felicity H*, a cockerel crowed suddenly and loudly, if unable to help himself. And from the sheltering trees of Mawr Wood and the island, birds were singing as if the day had started all over again, a bright new dawn.

The Commander relit his briar, the smoke from it drifting out over the water the colour of the haze on the hills. From above him came the snickering calls of a party of mallard in flight, and upstream, from its nest in a sycamore, or from the fishing shallows there, the rasping cry of a heron reached downriver. Sunlight drizzled on the water, the fishes ringing the surface, rising for the flies the Commander knew were hatching as he watched a couple of swallows hawking low on the wing. He knew his river, the home he and Priny had found over ten years before, when they were on their way to nowhere in particular, with nowhere in particular to go, coming to it by accident one winter's morning, with the scent of log fires over the village, and the welcoming doors of the Steamer Inn just opening.

They knew it then, knew they had found what they'd been looking for, even without altogether realising that they *had* been looking for it. A bit of old England, whichever of the two countries it or they happened to be in, and tied up on its river the hidden wonders of four Victorian paddle steamers in quite dotty, amiable decline.

When they learned that the *Batch Castle* was unoccupied they immediately put in a bid for it, using what was left from a venture farming edible snails in Cornwall, and the general just as immediately accepted. The Cunninghams had come home.

Miss Wyndham was telling them about one of her Siamese cats which had gone into elegant decline for a while after a narrow escape from under the wheels of a tractor.

"At least, that's what she told Jasmine," Miss Wyndham went on with a knowing smile. "But she's such a melo*dramatic* animal. Frankly, I didn't believe a word of it. She does so *like* to be centre stage."

"She's certainly *up*stage," the Commander said. "I always feel I ought to back from her presence."

"Oh, she's a *dreadful* snob," Miss Wyndham agreed. "Although," she added on a gossipy note, leaning forward in her chair, "just between ourselves, she may not have all that much to be snooty about. One doesn't like to be uncharitable, of course, but while one can certainly vouch for her being pure Siamese on her mother's side, one cannot really be sure who the father was. But I suppose for that I must share at least some of the blame by naming her Sheba."

Miss Wyndham paused, and leaning further forward peered intently at the Commander.

"Ah! I thought so! That eye is new, James."

"It came this morning, Harriet. Finally," the Commander said.

Shelly wasn't at all sure that she *did* want a proper look at it when the Commander offered, but Miss Wyndham was all for it, and he disappeared inside what was once the paddler's saloon and was now part of the living quarters.

He came out with a magnifying glass and wearing a black eye-patch.

The Commander held out his glass eye. "I gave it a swill first," he assured them.

Lieutenant Commander James Cunningham, DSO, SOC and Bar, RN (ret), a wartime Fleet Air Arm pilot, had lost an eye following the same accident that had shattered his leg, when a fellow Swordfish pilot, wounded and coming in after him, had crash landed, nose down, sending splinters from the wooden propellers scything across the aircraft carrier's deck.

He later commissioned a miniaturist to paint a collection of plain glass ones, depicting scenes from famous navel battles and landscapes that spoke of England, and one flying the Union Jack when a bit of swank, a bit of defiance in the face of whatever, was called for.

"It replaces Stubbs's *Huntsman and Horse*," he said, "which went overboard when I was giving it a bit of a polish on me sleeve. Careless of me. I rather liked that one, had a nice dash of colour to it. Both Ffion and Daniel, Phineas's boy, were good enough to go down and look for it, but both came up empty. Perhaps a trout swallowed it. Owain tells me they'll eat anything. And if so, I like to think that, say, one of his more successful clients caught the fish, took it home for supper, and as neither he nor his wife had need of a glass eye, it was given to their young boy to play marbles with."

"Remarkable!" Miss Wyndham said, peering at it through the magnifying glass. "Quite remarkable. And as with others, such detail."

"Gee!" Shelly said despite herself, when it came to her turn.

"An extraordinarily brilliant miniaturist called Michael Clay paints them for me," the Commander told her. "A man who can reduce the world to the tip of the smallest paint brush. Keeps him sane, he tells me. Except when it doesn't. And then he paints nothing but cats, usually orange ones, for a few months. The reason I had to wait so long for it."

"It's a sea battle," Shelly said.

"Indeed it is, Shelly!" the Commander agreed. "*The* sea battle. Trafalgar. Painted by Turner, as if from the mizzen shrouds of *HMS Victoria*, Admiral Nelson's flagship. Tra *–falgar!*" he said again, with a growl, unfurling the syllables like a battle pendent. "The greatest battle between ships of sail ever, and the most decisive in history. It put paid to Napoleon's plans to invade England and gave him a taste of his future – Waterloo! We were up against the allied fleets of Spain and France, but given our superior seamanship and the quality of our officers and men, the odds of course were still in our favour. They lost eighteen vessels to us, and not a single ship of ours saw the bottom. Not a single ship!"

The Commander fell silent, head back regarding them, his good eye mournful.

"But we did suffer a most grievous loss that day. Admiral Nelson fell, mortally wounded, on the quarter deck of the *Victory*," he said, sharing the news as if he had only just received it. "The

Admiral was assassinated. Brought down by a musket ball, fired by a cowardly Frenchie, skulking in the rigging of the *Redoubtable*."

The Commander took his eye back and removed the patch. His hands moved like a conjurer's over the empty socket and he blinked hard.

"God spared the admiral long enough for him to learn from his flag captain, Hardy, that they had taken the day. 'I have done my duty. I thank God for it,' Nelson said."

The Commander clamped his mouth round his briar pipe as if putting a stopper on his emotions, moved as he always was by the words. He blinked again and a tear leaked from his good eye. He searched hurriedly in the pockets of his ducks for his handkerchief.

Miss Wyndham caught her breath. "Duty! What a *splendid* word that is!" she exclaimed, jowls shaking, and sniffed back tears of her own.

They were both quite cuckoo, of course, Shelly thought, but they were her dear old cuckoos, her people now. And quick to tears as she was to laughter, and without having the remotest idea why, she added some of hers to theirs as she hugged them both in turn.

A few minutes later the Commander watched the first lieutenant making her way across to them with Annie Owen, their heads together, busy, no doubt, with a bit of local gossip.

He smiled at her, unseen and largely unaware he was doing so. It was, as he had said before, even after all these years, a pleasure still to see her walk into a room. Or, in this case, out of one. They were returning from the kitchen at the stern of the boat, carrying between then a replenished ice-bucket and the two bottles of home-made wine Annie had stored in the fridge when she'd arrived.

Annie's home-made wine, up to her elbows in the blood of the country, arms stained with blackberries, dewberries, raspberries, dog rose and plum, and all the other fruit of fields and hedgerows.

Elderberry flowers in this case, swags of them brought home last summer tied to her bicycle, providing squash for the children, the stems used as pea shooters and fuel for a winter stove, and wine, wine as clean tasting as water on stone and as delicate as Chablis.

The spare bottle was screwed into the ice-bucket, light swilling in it briefly, last year's sunshine, and the Commander got to work on the other with the Popeye novelty corkscrew, a birthday present from Phineas Cook.

He and Priny had first met in Southampton during the last war, when he'd been hospitalised there and she was back in Blighty after nursing through the air raids on Malta.

She was new to the ward and the staff nurse in attendance that day when the surgeon, with an entourage of earnest young doctors, had told him he had been unable to save his eye.

And she'd winked at him. Standing to one side of the group around his bed, she had flashed him a discreet, friendly wink of reassurance. Or else, he'd thought hopefully, she was terribly forward. Either way, he had scarcely heard a word the fellow had said after that.

Priny, in her maddeningly sexy uniform, the starched cuffs and cap, and black stockings, breezily bringing the outside world in with her each time she came on duty like a window flung open, reminding him that he was still there, still young and alive, with the world still out there, waiting for him.

Priny fitted another cigarette into a long-stemmed amber holder, and elegantly blew out smoke. She was wearing what she called her mad old bag spectacles, emerald green with two electric-blue butterflies perched, wings spread, on the frames, a prawn-pink nautical-style straw hat with a black ribbon, a vermilion silk shirt, matching her lipstick and nail extensions, red and white striped bell bottoms and red canvas deck shoes.

"All ripe and lovely," the Commander said of the wine, pouring it.

Shelly finished a second glass and said she wouldn't have another, thanks, she had an order of Conies to make up. Conies, Coney Island Specials, were frankfurters, quite ordinary hot-dogs served with diced onions, and then turned into something not at all ordinary by the addition of a secret recipe, a pickled relish, a family heirloom Shelly had brought with her across the Atlantic.

Shelly's Conies were now popular as far afield as the police station in Kingham. Made and served in the kitchen of Batch Hall, another money-making idea for the estate, along with bed and breakfast, and bingo on Tuesday and Thursday evenings in the servants' hall, with an added chance of a jackpot on the one-armed bandits bought second hand from an amusement arcade in Rhyl.

Almost immediately after Shelly had gone, Jasmine said that she had to be off, too; she had a client due for a reading. Jasmine did psychic readings on bingo nights at the Hall as well, splitting her fees fifty-fifty with the estate.

And then it was Annie's turn, off to get Owain, her husband, a bite of lunch. Owain was out on the river with a fishing client.

"You can't beat the *S S Batch Magna* when giving way together. Even Phineas is doing his bit," the Commander said, and frowned.

"Changed man all round lately, our Phineas is. Love of a good woman, see," Annie said, referring to Sally, Phineas's latest girlfriend. "Working hard, he was, when I dropped in earlier. *And,* as you say, James, he's volunteered to do this punting business."

"Ye – es," the Commander said doubtfully.

"This punting business" was advertised as a romantic, lantern-lit trip for two on the Cluny. Wine was also advertised as being available, and it was that combination of wine, Phineas, and some romantically inclined female, even one romantically inclined towards someone else, which caused the Commander to frown again.

Chapter Five

The only thing Phineas Cook was busy pounding away on at that moment were the tyres of his Frogeye, an old canary-yellow Austin Healey Sprite, parked up outside the moorings of his boat, the *Cluny Belle*, in Upper Ham.

He'd checked the oil and water and was now doing the tyres, while Bill Sikes, a large white boxer with the face of the spike-collared dog in a cartoon backyard, panted quietly with expectation in the passenger seat and kept an eye on him.

Phineas walked round the car, giving them a kick with the furtive air of a man kicking someone else's tyres.

He knew he shouldn't be out there. Where he should be, with a deadline and a new life to make a start on, was at work, at his typewriter. Instead of taking a day off as if earning a living was something only other people had to worry about. And it was just the other evening, sitting with Sally on her sofa, he'd said all those things about knuckling down to it, producing more work and therefore more income. He had, he'd said sternly, the future to think of now, a new start at things waiting.

And he had meant every word of it at the time. He'd felt big and brave under her serious, sweet gaze and spoke of big and brave things, like stability and responsibility. Doing so with the odd nervous laugh, coming as near as he'd come in a long time to making a commitment, while Sally sat holding his hand through it.

And now he was off on a day's jaunt. He did not, he told himself, deserve her.

He'd been restless since getting up this morning. It was that sort of day. With a thin mist on the water after the rain, and the sun rising behind it, burning it off, the river steaming under it. A day smoky with promise under an Eton-blue sky, carrying a memory of other, perfect, summers, spent carelessly on another river, of a time when it was always jolly boating weather. Always, as he remembered it, the Fourth of June, and there were strawberries and champagne when the shade was off the trees, and he wore a straw hat decked with flowers.

The day calling him back, calling him on the road to somewhere, anywhere, as long as it wasn't where he was now.

Because on such a day as this, even Batch Magna couldn't hold him.

Sitting at his worktable on deck, writing as Warren Chase the crime writer, he'd plodded grimly on for a while at his typewriter, cooped up with DI MacNail in a stuffy interview room at New Scotland Yard, where a bank clerk sweated across the table from him. He was the inside man on the latest bank raid by a South London mob, a bit player in a dangerous game, and one who was on the edge, MacNail knew, of fingering Mr Big.

Smiling with menace, MacNail, who, according to Warren Chase, had eyes the colour of rust on barbed wire, and a Glasgow kiss, a razor stripe, down one cheek, had pushed him that bit nearer and waited for him to crack.

And then, with the bank clerk about to cough, Warren Chase got up and went for another walk round the deck.

He became increasingly distracted as the sun climbed higher.

Until he heard only its bright music, calling with such promise he felt that if he listened hard enough he would be able to make out the words.

He reversed at speed until the Frogeye had room to turn, and then shot up past the pub and into the High Street, simply because that was the road he normally took when leaving the village. He had no idea where he was going, and knew that it didn't matter anyway. Because he'd never get there, wherever it was.

Wherever he ended up at times like this, it was never the place he'd started out for. Whatever the day, this sort of day, promised, whatever was going on out there, in that golden distance where summer is always perfectly summer, it was the sort of thing that was *always* going on somewhere else.

With Bill Sikes sticking his head out into the slipstream and taking bites out of the wind, the little yellow sports car sped up through the valley as if to a fire.

Chapter Six

Jasmine Roberts, meanwhile, dressed in purple silk printed with stars and moons, rainbows and comets, was waiting on the deck of her boat, the *Cluny Queen*, for her client to arrive.

She saw the car pull up at the gate of the mooring, and watched as the woman, middle-aged, expensively dressed and immaculately blonde, made her way gingerly up the ribbed wooden gangway on high heels.

Silly cow! I told her I lived on a boat, she thought. "You found us all right then, Mrs Yorke?" she said.

"I've visited the village before," the woman said, her voice husky. Gin and tears, Jasmine thought. Maybe that was why she was wearing the dark glasses. Or the old man had clocked her one.

"Oh, well, you'd know then. Lovely day it is now, isn't it? Beautiful it is – *beau*tiful," Jasmine said, as if about to start singing it. "Got a full line of washing out, I have. Think I'll put the baby out as well, a bit later," she added, and somewhere inside that large frame laughter rumbled, her body in the loose silk dress quivering, and then shaking with it like an engine catching.

"In the pushchair, I mean!" she managed to gasp. "In her pushchair! Not on the washing line!"

She doubled up with laughter, and unable to speak further, waved the woman aboard as if seeing a car back. "Oh, dear!" she wheezed, wiping at her eyes with a hand. "Oh, dear!"

Jasmine's children and their friends were everywhere. Running around the deck and jumping off it, screaming as if abandoning ship into the river, out on the moorings, in the den there built by one of her boyfriends, and on the swing and the log see-saw, and in the sand pit. A battle raged on the bank below the houseboat, the air loud with the sounds of exploding hand-grenades and deadly rapid fire, made by a gang of small boys with bloodthirsty imaginations and toy guns. While Jasmine's two toddlers, the twin girls, sat solemnly among it all on deck, at a round white plastic table and chairs from another of Bryony Owen's catalogues, splashing powder paint onto large sheets of paper and themselves.

Jasmine led her visitor through an open doorway hung with a rope of gold-coloured bells, into the sitting room, where more toys littered the floor and an incense stick burned.

The small room, which had once been the boat's saloon, accommodated a Welsh dresser laid with china and glass, a sideboard, a large sofa, two armchairs, a couple of hard chairs, an onyx coffee table, and a television. Highly polished, small brass ornaments, and a delicate china world of bonnets and crinoline stood with photographs of the children on every available surface, and there were ornamental plates, along with more photographs, and samples of the children's artwork, on the walls and martingale straps of polished leather and painted brass decorating the upright support timbers.

On top of a wood-burning stove which, on the *Cluny Queen*, stood in front of the two riverside windows, a small forest of wild flowers sprouted from an earthenware jug that had once held cider. Through the open windows drifted the excited chat-ter of more children, two boys, out with fishing rods in a pram dinghy.

"Sit down, dear," Jasmine said, moving a pile of clothes waiting to be ironed, a used cereal bowl, a bumper packet of disposable nappies, a couple of goose eggs Annie Owen had dropped in earlier, more toys and children's books, a few magazines and the TV Times, and a large, overweight white and ginger cat, to make space on the sofa.

Jasmine held onto the cat as if wondering where to put it, and then said, "You can go out, Sulta! It's time you got some fresh air. There's nothing wrong with you, there isn't."

The animal sagged, dangling lifelessly, bonelessly, in her hands. "Malingering, he is," she told her visitor. "He's got the end of a bit of an old cold, that's all. But oh, no, dying, he is. *Dy*ing. Typical male. Overrun, we are, with rats in the bilges, and he just lies there. They'll be up here soon, they will, pulling his tail. Well, I've told him, warned him, I have. If he doesn't get off his bum soon and do something about it I'm going to skin him. Turn him into a nightie case and feed the rest to that old pike out there. He can't get it past me, and he knows it. Don't you, you lazy animal. I'm a pet psychic, as well, dear, see," Jasmine explained, after putting the cat out. "Oh, yes, heard it all in my time, I have."

Mrs Yorke smiled wanly. She was in beige and cream, linen skirt and silk blouse, and the triple string of plump pearls around her neck were real. She sat gathered in on the edge of her seat, an island of herself, of who she was, among the disorder and council house bric-a-brac, her hands with their long, perfectly shaped fuchsia nails moving on the top of the handbag on her lap.

She had taken her dark glasses off and Jasmine saw that she wasn't hiding a black eye, that it was worse than that. That there was another sort of pain there, the pain, she thought, of loss. Her eyes were brittle with it and her face, with its model bone structure, looked swollen with tears, her make-up, which Jasmine suspected was heavier than she normally wore, like a dressing on a wound.

Out on deck one of the girls was singing as she skipped, her feet beating out the rhythm.

Church Myddle Chronicle, Kingham News,
Did you ever see a cat in a pair of shoes?

Jasmine closed the door.

"You know I'm not a medium, don't you, dear," she said gently. "I'm a clairvoyant, not a medium. People do make that mistake."

"I don't need a medium, he's not dead yet," the woman said, trying, awkwardly, to make light of it. "But you do … well, *predictions,* don't you?" she asked, looking up at Jasmine, as if amused by it.

"You could call them that, dear, yes," Jasmine said. But she knew then that she hadn't got the sort of future Mrs Yorke wanted.

Jasmine's knowledge of chirognomy, taken from one of the books in her bedroom, told her that the shape of Mrs Yorke's hands came under the classification of the Philosophical Hand. It told her that, if Mrs Yorke was typical, then she was a calculator, someone in whom reason, even in love, was likely to prevail.

Which, she thought wryly, was just as well.

Because she now knew a lot more than that about Mrs Yorke. And from a place where the real work came from, the stuff that she didn't have to read up on, or guess at.

She knew it dimly and piece by piece, like gossip heard a while ago and which was now coming back to her. She knew that Mrs Yorke had married for money. She knew that she had a much younger lover and that she had been reduced to gratitude by the affair. Grateful for what he pretended to give her, what she paid him to give her, and had been happy for a while to believe he meant. And now that part of her which despaired, unsleeping in the small hours or alone with herself in the bathroom mirror, which saw the bargaining involved, the lies that money bought, wanted to be told it wasn't so.

Mrs Yorke, Jasmine knew, had come late to life. She was learning only now that simply because she wanted a thing didn't always mean she could have it. She was grieving for that, for who she had once been. For lost youth and looks, for age-ing, and, perhaps for the first time, for love.

She was a silly, selfish, spoilt, immature women. And Jasmine's heart, which rarely judged, went out to her.

"Like a cup of tea, dear?" she said.

Before the woman could answer, bumps and screams came from the uptops, as the children's two bedrooms, built on top of the deck living quarters, were called. Mrs Yorke watched bemused as Jasmine grabbed a carpet sweeper and thumped hard on the ceiling with it, dislodging a couple more children, their footsteps running down the companionway to the deck. And from the depths of an armchair, where she'd crawled after playing, Jasmine's one-year-old daughter stirred and bawled.

"Oh, blimey! I'd forgotten about her!"

Jasmine removed her necklace and tossed it from her, caught up in a sudden drama of an abandoned baby, and took her on her lap.

"There, there, little heart, little plum, pert bach! There, there, there," she cooed, popping the top buttons of her dress like peas, and heaving out a breast which wriggled for a moment in her hand like a large freckled fish.

Her daughter fastened lustily on a rose-brown nipple and closed her eyes.

Jasmine smiled tenderly at the feeding head.

"She'll go down again in a minute, bless her. Then I'll make us some tea."

Jasmine thought of her powers, her real powers, as coming from a fifth element, a quintessential world that was everywhere but for most people remained just out of sight. Something there and then not there, something almost remembered and then almost instantly forgotten. A moment of sudden, releasing happiness out of nowhere, or something caught out of the corner of an eye, or felt somewhere behind them, a split second before they turned to look. For Jasmine it was just outside the door.

An unimaginable world she imagined, believed she had been led to imagine, as being like the air above a great river, the almost wordless voices from there which told her things, as free and as fleet in that element as fishes. And which teased her sometimes about that, giggling then like children, effortlessly just out of reach, catch me if you can.

And she knew that one day she would. She had no doubt that that world existed. Everything else to Jasmine was a struggle upstream until we got there. That was coming home.

A few minutes later she watched her baby daughter slump into sleep again off her breast, and put her in her pushchair, ready for Mrs Yorke.

She wouldn't offer her hope, she wouldn't do that to her. But she would try to send her home with some sort of future. And she didn't need her voices for that. Just tea and talk, while Jasmine listened. Tea and sympathy, and a few more tears.

She went and put the kettle on.

Chapter Seven

While Phineas, roaring off up through the lanes, didn't mind where he was going, as long as it wasn't where he was, Owain Owen wasn't going anywhere *but* where he was – ever again!

Owain had lived away from his village only twice in his life. The first time in the last war, when he wore the uniform of a rifleman of the Welsh Borderers, among the first to volunteer to fight for his country, even, generously, the half of it that was in England. And again last year, when in Batch Magna, a place where nothing ever happened, nothing ever changed, except the seasons, suddenly everything changed, with the death of the old squire, and, through the law of entailment, the arrival of the new, an American, with plans to bring Batch Magna into the modern world. Which meant, among other things, a scheme to build a holiday village on the river.

Owain and his family, along with the residents of the other houseboats, on the receiving end of eviction notices, found themselves banished from their river, from their home, exiled to a rented cottage in Little Batch, three miles upstream. A move of such dislocation that Owain neither spoke, except in a whisper, as if at the doctor's, as Annie had put it, nor removed his jacket except to wash or for bed for the entire, mercifully short, time they were there.

Owain had long forgiven Sir Humph for that business, they all had. And for his part, Sir Humph had long forgiven them for plotting his demise, planning to murder him over it. Because then it had all changed again, when Humphrey, engaged to another and with Batch Magna's shiny new future in his executive briefcase, had run into Clem.

Owain never quite seemed able to grasp why they had to leave the river, and never fully seemed for a while to grasp how they were able to return there. Back on the *Felicity H,* it was a week before he'd take off his jacket there as well, and to talk above a whisper, as if at the doctor's, as if not wanting to draw attention to the fact that they *were* back there.

Owain, with his favourite bamboo rod, was fishing for the results of the trout fry he'd introduced to the river last year, sitting with his collie, Bryn, and a fishing client on a Wyre punt that a few months ago had willow herb growing out of it on the *Felicity H's* mooring. Owain had patched it up and re-tarred it, a work for him of love, and hope.

His and Annie's roots in this place went deep. Generations of both families had worked for the estate. Owain in his time under the general had been both a water bailiff and keeper, and now, serving it again as ghillie, was back to where his heart was.

Owain could barely read or write. His stories were in the sounds, signs and tracks of the woods and fields, and the things he read in the colour of the river and its weather, things which told him the best way to fish it, a likely eddy he'd spotted, the slack water between currents where a chub might be keeping station, or a slight darkening of a spot which meant a bream was down there, scouring the mud on the bed, and the movement of animals on its banks.

From among the green flowers of an island of sweet grass, several black fluffy moorhen chicks followed their parents upstream, their legs furiously busy underwater, the survivors, Owain knew, of a spring raid by a fox on their nest among the grass. Swallows and wagtails fed on the air above the water, and from upstream, where its nest was lodged like flood debris in the top branches of a sycamore, a heron flapped low over it, snacking on dragonflies.

The sky and the tops of the big hawthorns on Snails Eye Island, from where doves called, endlessly, vibrated gently in the water, the air washed with the smell of weed and the river turning to silver and white over the fish weir downstream, and scented with meadowsweet. The sun glinted on the glossy new green of the willows and the water meadows were in bloom, golden with marsh marigolds, and sown with bright patches of scabious, ragged robin and cuckoo flower.

And Owain could *not* imagine a more perfect place, a more perfect world.

'By the river and with it and on it and in it, it's brother and sister to me, and aunts and company, and food and drink. It's my world and I don't want any other.' Phineas Cook had quoted that to him, or something like it, out of some book or other, and he'd been much taken by it. Whoever had said it, Owain knew *exactly* what they meant.

It's my world and I don't want any other.

He cocked an ear, as sharp as a water rat's when it suited him, as his wife, Annie, had pointed out more than once, picking up a series of short, sharp whistles from the direction of the island and the otter holt there. The female, with food waiting or the smell of danger on the air, calling her young. The female that the Commander reckoned was the spirit of the late general, when she was first seen after an absence of such animals from that stretch of water for ten years or more, appearing only when Batch Magna and its river were threatened. And then, after driving off the dog otter when he had served his purpose, staying to watch over them again.

Something which Owain accepted without question. He knew that otters had magical powers, everyone did, except of course an Englishman – as long as that Englishman wasn't the Commander. But then, to Owain's mind, which did things differently, the Commander wasn't really an Englishman, but a Welshman who just happened to be English.

But what he hadn't understood was why the general had chosen to return as a *female* otter.

Until, that is, the day on the *Felicity H,* when Annie, watching the cubs through the glasses playing on the island, had wondered aloud if Clem was pregnant yet.

The penny had dropped then, all right. And after that, for reasons he didn't fully understand, and didn't bother trying to, he had felt more secure than he'd felt since returning from Little Batch, had felt since then that he really *was* back home, with the door closed behind him, shut firmly on that time.

He spotted the darting red of a male stickleback, zigzagging in a mating dance, getting ready to spawn one of the many females he'd get through in a season.

Randy little bugger, he thought, and wondered if Annie was free for an hour after lunch.

Chapter Eight

Humphrey, meanwhile, was on his way to buy Tower Bridge, or at any rate a part of it.

He was strolling carelessly through Westminster, heading for the House of Commons, a sparkle to the morning air from the broad sweep of the Thames, carrying all that history on its shoulders, and Big Ben, obligingly striking the hour above him, black cabs, and red buses shining in the sun like the money box he had as a child, the model of a Number 9 Routemaster he never saw full, his nickels and dimes never managing to reach the top deck before being raided by his mom to help with the groceries. On the bus of Humphrey's childhood, there was always 'plenty of room on top'.

Chomping on a Havana torpedo, and wearing tartan seersucker pants and a shirt with parrots on it, he managed to suggest a visitor from a place far more foreign than either America or Batch Magna, far more foreign even than Hawaii, where his shirt came from. A man with knowledge of a place where everything that one could reasonably want or need did indeed grow on trees, and was there for the picking. Looking with benevolence on London as it hurried past, giving the impression of a man quite prepared to share that knowledge if ever London slowed down long enough to listen.

He was aware that it was here, in Westminster, that the adventure that was the Cluny Steamboat Company had first set sail, when his forebear Sir Cosmo Strange, in London for a much needed discussion about the estate's finances with his accountants, returned instead with five paddle steamers.

The side-wheeler vessels had been part of a fleet plied by London County Council like omnibuses between Hammersmith and Greenwich. And when Sir Cosmo first clapped eyes on one, paddling and puffing her way busily upstream, he was instantly and completely smitten, the thunderous beasts of the London and Birmingham Railway, his erstwhile love, discarded without a second thought for the trim lines and saucy bustle of a Thames paddle steamer.

He spent what time he could when in town riding up and down river on their trembling decks, in thrall to their steamy, sooty beauty. To the slap of the wheels and their churned wash, and the gleaming splendours of the engine room, the beating, oiled heart of the boat, hearing, in the clamour of a twin-cylinder compound diagonal engine, the music of the spheres.

And then on the morning he was due to meet the estate's accountants, sitting with coffee in his club after fortifying himself for the ordeal with a full English breakfast, he read in the ironed pages of *The Times*, read as if he were meant to, that after two years of steadily falling receipts, the LCC had decided to put the entire fleet under the hammer.

The accountants were immediately forgotten.

He was among the first at the public auction on Westminster Pier, coming on all thirty of the vessels tied up along the river there on that mid-December day, his eyes wide at the sight. Christmas, for Sir Cosmo, had come early.

He bid successfully for five of them, the smallest of the fleet, paying in total nearly six thousand pounds. And could only wonder that money, mere money, could buy such things.

Not that Sir Cosmo had any money, or none to spare, but scribbling busily on the back of an envelope, he had gazed with satisfaction at the result. Arithmetic wasn't his strong point, but even he could see that, whatever it came to, ferrying people, goods and livestock between Batch Magna and, say, Shrewsbury added up to a good deal of profit, whichever way you looked at it.

He worked out how he was going to pay for them on the other side of the envelope, selling off another slice of his estate there.

He telegraphed for a team of estate workers to entrain for London, to be instructed with him in the mysteries, the wondrous mysteries, of a paddle steamer, with talk of connecting rods, valve gears, steam and boiler pressures, dampers, crankshafts and pistons, regulators and relief taps, bringing Sir Cosmo to a state of near ecstasy.

With one of his keepers acting as fireman, he took the wheel of the biggest of the five paddlers, earmarked for his flagship and already renamed the *Felicity H* after his wife, in an attempt to divert the awkward questions no doubt waiting for him.

Sir Cosmo's hand never strayed for long from his very own steam whistle as he led his small flotilla upriver to Gravesend, to the River Medway and dry dock at Chatham, where they were partially dismantled and hauled over to the railhead on steel rollers for the train to Shrewsbury, pulled there by an engine called *Progress*.

In Shrewsbury, they were put back together in a Severn boat-yard, and their fires relit for the thirty-odd mile journey down that river to Batch Magna and the home waters of the River Cluny, where the village was hung with bunting and the flags of two countries flown, and the Silver Band from Church Myddle, waiting on the hay wharf, soon to become the landing stage of the Cluny Steamboat Company, played them home.

And Humphrey felt now that he marched with the spirit of Sir Cosmo.

He decided that one of the bridge's towers would fit nicely on what used to be a couple of tennis courts in the grounds of the Hall. Like his forebear Humphrey had also done his sums, and if this wasn't a money spinner in the making, then he didn't know one when he saw it. A pound sterling entry fee for adults and half price for kids.

They'll be queuing up as far as the High Street.

He frowned. He had to be businesslike about this, had to ask himself what use was the tower without one of the steam engines used to power the bascules the guy mentioned to go with it. And then, to go with the steam engine, he'd need a bascule to play with, wouldn't he, one of the arms that go up and down, *and* an accumulator, to make the set? Right? *Right!*

He'd let the Commander have first go.

Tower Bridge, he had learned, was hydraulically operated using steam to power the pumping engines, the energy built up by them was then stored in massive accumulators. He'd been given the low-down on it that morning by the guy from Her Majesty's Bridges, or whatever it was, while Clem was window shopping in the West End. And boy, wasn't she in for a surprise when she got back!

Humphrey had met the man earlier, when gazing dreamily up at the bridge, wearing his Yankees baseball cap, a camera slung round the neck of his Hawaiian shirt, and licking a large cornet of knickerbocker glory. He'd visited the Tower of London again after Clem had left their hotel for the shops, for another round of beheadings, torture and dungeons, and then wandered down to the bridge.

"A remarkable feat of engineering, what?" the man had said at his ear.

Humphrey started guiltily.

He hadn't been looking at a remarkable feat of engineering. He'd been looking at a castle, seeing a castle in the ornate Victorian heights of the bridge, with standards rippling from the battlements, and damsels and jousting and all that, and a story about a knight rescuing a princess from a tower, and men with black crosses on their shields thundering out in pursuit over the drawbridge, licking steadily at his ice-cream and watching it all as if at the movies.

He made up for it by not only agreeing that it was a remarkable feat of engineering, but adding with a judicious air that he reckoned it was probably the *best* remarkable feat of engineering he'd ever seen, and narrowing his eyes at the structure as if making a few tentative calculations, wondered how much it weighed.

"Well," the man said on a laugh, "I'm not sure that that's ever been computed. It's an interesting question, nevertheless. And not one I have to confess we get asked all that often. What I *can* tell you is that eleven thousand tons of iron went in to providing the towers and walkways, which were then clad in Cornish granite and Portland stone, so that should give you some idea."

He took a fob watch from a waistcoat pocket and snapped it open. "And if you're here in roughly three hours from now, it's scheduled to break-to, to use the terminology, for a freighter. They'll be opening fully then, that's to say the bascules, the arms of the bridge, will be raised the maximum eighty-six degrees to allow passage. A procedure which, despite the complexity of the operation, takes, believe it or not, a mere sixty seconds, using the on-tap energy stored in six accumulators. The accumulators, massive affairs, feed the driving engines, you see, which in turn power the bascules."

Humphrey had stopped licking his ice-cream and his mouth was open.

His companion chuckled. "Yes, that's right," he said, answering a question Humphrey hadn't asked, "you've guessed it. For my sins, I'm a civil servant. Specifically, a civil servant with responsibility for Her Majesty's Bridges. H. M. Bridges, as the department, rather more prosaically, is known."

He took a slim silver case from an inside pocket.

"My card," he said, and Humphrey read that he was being addressed by a Mr Charles St-John Pawsley, Operations Executive for Her Majesty's Public Works (Bridges Division).

Mr St-John Pawsley wore a bowler hat and a pinstripe suit, and carried a black leather document case and a furled umbrella. He was also wearing an Old Etonian tie. Humphrey knew it was an Old Etonian tie because Phineas Cook wore one when on his way to see his bank manager, to go with what he called his overdraft suit. He also knew that in this country, guys who went to that school ended up as the movers and shakers, hotshot politicians, and captains of industry, and all that. Unless they were called Phineas Cook.

"Yes, it's a great pity," Mr St-John Pawsley said, taking his card back.

He looked up at the bridge and shook his head.

"A great pity. And I certainly shan't be the only one sorry to see it go. It does, after all, stand large in popular sentiment as the very gateway to London. A landmark recognised the world over. It has strode these banks since 1894, when it was erected under the auspices of the old Corporation of London, the body then responsible for this part of the river. It was designed by Horace Jones, you know, the corporation architect, in collaboration with one John Wolfe Barry. It took eight years and the labour of nearly five-hundred workers to construct it. It was at the time the largest and most sophisticated bascule bridge ever constructed. Bascule, as you doubtless know, is French for see-saw."

Humphrey didn't know, and had anyway been busy thinking about something else.

"Where's it going then? You said you wouldn't be the only one sorry to – "

"Yes, yes. Ah, I thought you might have known. It was fairly widely reported last week. The old boy's going to be pulled down. Replaced with a structure more suited not only to today's traffic, but looking ahead as one must, to the volume of a century and more from now. Not a decision we took lightly, I can assure you. We spent a whole year surveying it before deciding."

He pulled back then, as if to get a better look at Humphrey, and frowning enquiringly, asked if by any chance he was an American.

"Ah, I thought that might be the case," he said, when Humphrey admitted that he was. "The accent, you know. Well, I'm surprised you didn't see it advertised for sale over there. We like selling this sort of thing to our cousins in the States. You've already got the old London Bridge. As you doubtless know, it now sits on Arizona's Lake Havasu. It's that state's biggest tourist attraction after the Grand Canyon – an absolute *money* spinner, old boy. So, perhaps some other state will shrewdly follow suit. Otherwise, someone's going to make a killing buying it for scrap, the sort of price we're asking. Ridiculous really, but there you are. It's the royal charter, you know, limits the profit we're allowed to make."

Humphrey looked appalled. "Scrap …? What, junked?"

"Well, Her Majesty's Government can't just *give* it away."

"No, of course not. It's just that – well, it just seems a heck of a shame, that's all."

"Yes. Yes, it is rather. An inglorious end to an old friend left behind by modern times, by a London that has no further use for it. It has done the capital and its river some service, some service. It has stood steadfast against tides and storm, against Zeppelins, the bombs of the Luftwaffe and the attentions of the IRA. It has opened its arms to the trading nations of the world and carried Londoners in their tens of thousands on its back all these years, feeding each morning the beating heart of this great city, and bearing them home again when their day is done. As is the old boy's now," Mr St-John Pawsley said, removing his bowler and placing it briefly over his heart. "As is his now," he added on a dying fall.

"Still," he went on briskly, putting his hat back on and giving the crown a businesslike tap, "the march of time, and all that, you know. But perhaps someone will put in an offer, turn it into a tourist attraction – after all, the asking price is nominal, a mere token."

Humphrey was staring up at the red, white and blue heights of the bridge, his meaty features set and stubborn looking, and as if tears weren't far away. Both Clem and his mom knew that look. It usually meant he thought something small and vulnerable was in trouble, not, as in this case, eleven thousand tons of old iron.

But Humphrey knew what it felt like to be large and unwanted. If he could have done so he would have bought it, all of it, there and then.

"How much is it, then?" he asked, and wondered where he was going to put it.

"Mmm …?"Mr St-John Pawsley murmured, also gazing up and as if lost in thought.

"You said it was a mere token, or something. How much is that?"

"Well, the figure is yet to be ratified, of course – Her Majesty's Civil Service, you know," he said with a chuckle. "But I can tell you that any prospective buyer should think of something in the order of fifty thousand pounds sterling. Yes, sir, you did hear me correctly, a mere fifty thousand pounds sterling. And not only that, if sold to America, a reduction of ten thousand pounds is involved. And *if* sold to America, then shipping is thrown in – gratis and absolutely free. Although I should add," he cautioned, "that the cost of re-erection must, of course, be borne by the purchaser."

"Yeah. Yeah, of course," Humphrey said.

"But, even so, as I say, it's a snip at the price, a giveaway, as I believe you say in your country. Her Majesty's Government is, as ever, eager to sugar relations with your administration.

A state of affairs which some lucky US citizen or corporation is set to profit hugely from. Still, that's diplomacy for you," he added, and snapped off another look at his fob. "Well, no rest for the wicked. It's been a pleasure, sir, talking to you."

"I couldn't afford to buy all of it and anyway I don't know where I'd put it," Humphrey said in a rush.

Mr St-John Pawsley frowned.

"My dear sir," he said sternly, "I haven't suggested that you *do* buy it. Any of it. I daren't. There are strict rules governing that sort of thing, you know. *Very* strict rules."

He hesitated, and then smiled as if relenting.

"But, well, I suppose there's no harm in telling you that the official description of sale refers to the whole or *part* thereof. One of the towers, say."

"How much would that be, one of the towers?"

"Five grand," Mr St-John Pawsley said immediately, lowering his voice and glancing around. "Five thousand pounds sterling. With, as I say, free shipping thrown in."

"I'll take one," Humphrey heard himself say.

Chapter Nine

And now, after picking up his chequebook from the hotel, he was on his way to the House of Commons to pay for it, plus a steam engine, a bascule and an accumulator.

He hadn't worked out yet how to get it all home, or when there how to get it up again – but boy, won't Batch Magna be surprised when that turns up on its doorstep!

They were meeting at the House and not at Mr St-John Pawsley's Whitehall office because Mr St-John Pawsley was due to brief a cabinet minister, and was likely to be tied up all day there. Humphrey had decided to wrap the deal up first, hand over the cheque and tell the bank afterwards, when it was in the bag. This sort of deal had to be done with your foot down, as they say on Wall Street. Stop for a green light and you'll find yourself left behind in the traffic with all the other losers.

He moved the cigar round his mouth, and working on the price Mr St-John Pawsley had put on a tower, came up with a ballpark figure of not more than twenty-five thousand grand sterling for the lot.

Not that he had twenty-five thousand grand sterling, or even the bargain-basement five grand sterling needed for the tower. But he had the Hall. He'd take a mortgage out on that. He wasn't *entirely* sure what taking out a mortgage meant, and had no idea at *all* how much the Hall might be worth. More than twenty-five thousand grand sterling, he was sure – a *lot* more, he wouldn't be at all surprised. It had any number of rooms for a start – he'd never been quite sure how many – and any number of outhouses, and some of its park left still, with peacocks and a boathouse at the end of a creek with boats in it, and lawns running down to the Cluny. It had paddlers sitting on the river, and Phineas, and Jasmine, and the Commander and Priny, and Annie and Owain, and old Tom Parr, and Miss Wyndham, and John Beecher with a cricket bat, and Pugh the Pew in the village shop, and Saturday nights in the Steamer with Patrick on the piano, and ...

He couldn't go on. He'd been homesick almost as soon as he'd arrived in London, and any more of that sort of stuff and he'd be collecting Clem and taking the next train back. Whatever it was, however much it might all be worth, he could only wonder, as his forebear had done when gazing on the paddle steamers, that money, mere money, could buy such things.

Mr St-John Pawsley had told him which entrance to use, and when there to ask one of the policemen on duty for the office of the Minister for Transport.

But when Humphrey arrived he was standing outside, waiting for him.

Mr St-John Pawsley, with a bank account set up in the name of H. M. Bridges, greeted him like an old friend, shaking his hand and telling him how delighted he was to see him again, his eyes gleaming like teeth. After weeks of trying to sell Tower bridge, or part thereof, turning up for it each day as if to the office, he had been about to write off the idea.

This would be Humphrey's second visit to the House of Commons. He'd done the tour with Clem the other day, had looked down on the green benches from the Strangers' Gallery, and been photographed in front of the statue of Sir Winston Churchill, an overweight guy who smoked cigars, and had learned that it wasn't Guy Fawkes who had led the Gunpowder

Plot but another conspirator and that Guy Fawkes had been left holding the matches. The guide at this point had asked him with a pained expression would he please mind *not* lighting his cigar.

Humphrey heeled out what was left of his Havana now, and walked in with Mr St-John Pawsley, through the stone hall echoing with the stern business of politics, busy with people scurrying about carrying important-looking papers, bringing the sun in with him and a flight of parrots.

Calling him old boy, Mr St-John Pawsley said that he was sorry, but the Cabinet minister wanted his office for what he, Mr St-John Pawsley, casually called a bit of paper shuffling with the Prime Minister. He was sure Humphrey would understand, he went on, sitting down on one of the public benches.

Humphrey's mouth was open again. The *Prime Minister*. He'd said he wouldn't call himself a hotshot again, not after last time, but if this wasn't hotshot stuff then perhaps some body would kindly tell him just what was!

He had made a decision on his way there. He'd come clean with the guy, shoot with a straight arrow – yes, he told him now, he was an American, but no, he did not live over there, so it wouldn't be right to claim the ten thousand grand sterling reduction. But he might ask for help in the shipping. If only, he added with a laugh, for somebody to point him in the right direction for Wales – the bit, that is, that was in England, and, he added with another laugh, the bit of England that was in Wales.

Mr St-John Pawsley, taking a sheaf of official-looking papers from his document case, paused.

Humphrey went on to tell him that his name was Humphrey, but to call him Humph. He was, as he'd said, an American, living half in England and half in Wales, what's called the Marches, and he was a baronet, going from a short-order cook living with his mom in a second-floor walk-up in the Bronx to Batch Hall, the manor house of a place he'd never heard of, after a great uncle he hadn't known he'd had died. And he was in London on honeymoon with Clem, his Clem, Lady Strange, as, chuckling about it, Humphrey supposed she was now.

Behind his faint polite smile Mr St-John Pawsley was busy wondering what he was listening to.

"So, anyways," Humphrey went on, "as well as the tower, I'll need a steam engine, if that's all right with you, and Her Majesty or whoever, a bascule to go up and down, and an accumulator, please, to make the set."

He grinned at Mr St-John Pawsley, his eyes utterly without guile, the meaty openness of his face waiting like a blank cheque.

And suspicion touched Mr St-John Pawsley like a hand on his collar.

He glanced casually round and wondered if the American was wired.

Whoever he was working for should have sent a better actor, and one with a far more convincing script. Nobody, or no adult at any rate, was *that* naïve, that innocent. The last time he remembered anyone looking at him like that was a nephew, and he was ten or so at the time. Mr St-John Pawsley hadn't been sure what he'd been listening to, but he knew what he should be looking at, he'd reeled it in enough times – the greed which, as far as he was concerned, made his marks as guilty as he was.

But this wasn't the face of a grown-up, rising for the bait of easy money. This was a ten-year-old talking about what he wanted Father Christmas to bring him.

Which was about the mental age of whoever had come up with his cover story. Far too much unnecessary and confusing detail – and the most outrageously unlikely story outside of an Odeon he'd ever heard. He felt professionally affronted.

The man had to be a plant, an agent provocateur. He could be working for the American authorities, after him still for selling, as the Senator for New York State, shares in the Statue of

Liberty to a group of Japanese businessmen, or maybe Scotland Yard. He was hardly unknown to the Fraud Squad, and he had been concerned that he'd been a little *too* busy on the bridge.

Humphrey said that he was going to put up the bit of Tower Bridge he wanted to buy in Batch Hall's grounds, and let somebody called the Commander have first go.

He told him about the other people who lived aboard Victorian paddle steamers that were now little homes, about a river called the Cluny and its village, Batch Magna, with a Miss Wyndham peddling up its High Street on a bicycle. And somebody called old Tom Parr, and Mr Pugh the shopkeeper, and John Beecher, a coalman, defending the honour of his village at a Saturday wicket, and tales of summer jollies, and boating and picnics, and days when the lamps were lit early on the river, and the owls called.

And while Humphrey burbled happily on, Mr St-John Pawsley sat beguiled.

He was no longer at all sure that Humphrey was a plant, and no longer much cared. He was taking a holiday from that life. It was such a warm, cosy, *safe* world he was listening to, like being tucked up and read to again by his old mum. Like being back in a time when *he* made a list of things he wanted Father Christmas to bring him. Back in a time when he believed still that there *was* a Father Christmas.

"Anyways, enough of me yapping on, let's hit a few figures round the ballpark, see where they land," Humphrey said then cheerfully.

He was enjoying himself now. He'd been a bit unsure of all this at first, shooting deals with top guns like Mr St-John Pawsley, using the House of Commons like an office, with talk of cabinet ministers shuffling papers down the hall with the PM, as he now thought of him, but this hotshot stuff was proving after all to be right up his street, no matter what anybody else thinks.

Mr St-John Pawsley, on the other hand, was steadily sinking deeper into a morass of gloom.

Scenes from his past went by as if glimpsed through the bars of a prison van, the journey from a life that still had Father Christmas in it to the banging of a cell door on his last helping of porridge. The judge who had been like an uncle to him over the years, peering down with disappointment through the curtains of his wig as he handed it out. And his old mum, sobbing into her handkerchief in her usual place on the public benches.

His old mum, who had always been there to greet him when he came out, with his little brown paper parcel and hopes for the future, growing old in her trust of his words when he spoke of how this really would be the last time, honest, and meaning it, then.

And now here he was again.

Even the sight of the chequebook sitting open on the bench between them, with a clean, blank page waiting to be filled in, failed to rouse him from the misery of remorse.

Humphrey, frowning with concern, asked if he was okay, and wondered if it was all right to give the Operations Executive for Her Majesty's Public Works (Bridges Division) a shoulder hug. He did that when his friends looked down. Phineas Cook, after such an embrace had left him unable to type for a couple of days, took care, no matter how he might feel, to put a smile on things when Humphrey was about.

Humphrey looking at him like that was the last straw for Mr St-John Pawsley.

Stuffing the transfer papers back in his document case, he muttered something on a choked note, and Humphrey's mouth fell open for a third time that morning as Mr St-John Pawsley leapt to his feet, threw a last, wild look at him, and with a sound like a sob made off in the direction of the exit.

Humphrey watched him go, chewing on his lower lip and wondering what it was he'd said.

He was still puzzling over it in bed in their hotel that night. He decided in the end, rather defensively, that it was probably the strain of being a hotshot that had finally got to the poor guy. So maybe he was better off not being a hotshot after all.

Anyway, tomorrow they'd be back in Batch Magna, and it didn't matter there whether you were a hotshot or not.

Although he and Clem had solemnly promised each other that there would in their marriage be no secrets between them, he had decided not to tell her about it. Because if it hadn't been the strain of being a hotshot but something he had said, then, well, he'd feel a bit guilty about it, about not telling her, but he didn't want her to know he'd goofed like that, that's all, stopped them having a real money spinner for the estate.

And Clem also decided that there were some secrets in a marriage that were best kept just that. He would never hear it from her lips about the dress she had seen in Bond Street, which they really couldn't afford, and which she had only being stopped from buying because they didn't have it in her size.

She snuggled up to him, feeling virtuous about it anyway. Especially as Humphrey had been rather sweetly at pains to assure her that *his* only expenditure of the morning had been a large cornet of knickerbocker glory.

And tomorrow she'd back in Batch Magna, they both would, safely removed from all temptation.

Chapter Ten

Miss Wyndham stopped off first at the village shop in the High Street, where the red dragon on the flag above the entrance spoke for Wales.

She leaned her bicycle against the whitewashed wall of the shop's small front garden, adjusted her thorn-proof skirt and stuffed a couple of escaped coils of hair back under a brown felt hat with a jay's feather in the band, while looking about her with an air of being mildly surprised to find herself there.

The bell of the door of the shop, which Mr Pugh relied on to alert him to sneak thieves, largely in the form of Jasmine Roberts's marauding gang up from the river, rang her in.

A few villagers were in a huddle at the post office counter, where Mrs Pugh sat, plump as a guinea pig, passing on the latest gossip with the stamps and postal orders. The rest of the shop, the domain of Mr Pugh, had one customer in it, waiting at the counter under a ceiling hung with dustbins, washing lines, buckets, brooms, stepladders, gardening tools, gumboots, pitchforks, hose pipes, timber saws and axes, while the shopkeeper emptied his basket. Taking his cue from the Imperial Stores supermarket in Kingham, where the tills never seemed to stop ringing, Mr Pugh had some time ago gone self-service.

Miss Wyndham's eyes narrowed when she saw that the customer was Colonel Ash.

"Ah, good morning, Colonel! *Lovely* day," she said with a sort of breezy openness. And someone with more perception than the Colonel possessed could have told him that here was a woman with something to hide.

Mr Pugh, thin, yellowing strands of hair plastered across his bony scalp like flattened winter grass, the nests of broken veins on his face glowing like coals after a recent visit to his store-room, glanced up slyly.

"It's going to rain again later, apparently," he slipped in.

The Colonel frowned. "Is that the forecast?"

"My barometer said it was set fair for the day. Mind you," Miss Wyndham admitted, more to herself, "it *always* says that."

"I caught the local chap on the wireless first thing," the Colonel said, "and I have to say that I don't recall any mention of rain."

Mr Pugh grinned, a servile show of large, ill-fitting teeth.

"Well, maybe it was yesterday I heard it, Colonel. Yesterday morning, like."

"It didn't rain yesterday either, not in any part of the day. Nor, again as I recall, was there any mention of it doing so in the morning." The Colonel sounded determined to get to the bottom of it.

Mr Pugh looked cornered.

"Well, perhaps it was the day before, then," he said placatingly.

"The day before …? That would be Tuesday …" The Colonel frowned, considering it.

"Or one day last week, maybe," Mr Pugh got in quickly. "Perhaps that's what I'm confusing it with. Yes. Yes, that would be it. One day sometime last week, it was."

"Hmm …"

The Colonel didn't look altogether convinced. But prepared to let the matter rest there, courteously insisted that Miss Wyndham be served first.

"And what can I do madam for this morning?" The shopkeeper said, and bared his teeth at her like a horse.

And Miss Wyndham caught a whiff of the Extra-Strong mints he used. Mr Pugh regularly punished a conscience schooled in the village's Methodist chapel by drinking in what he still thought of as secret, and had further torment waiting in Deuteronomy's Curses for Disobedience in a collection of top-shelf magazines hidden behind the canned soups.

Both of which activities had long been known to his wife and, through her, to the entire village and beyond.

Miss Wyndham asked for a quarter of a pound of her usual caramel fudge.

"*Ah* – ah, well, now, madam,"Mr Pugh said, a man with a surprise up his sleeve. "Well, now, it so happens that this morning I am in the position to offer in the fudge line several options – *several* options," he emphasised, "in addition to madam's usual requirement in that department. Old Mr Minton, who retired recently as confectionery representative," Mr Pugh went on, his teeth taking the syllables of the last couple of words like fences, "was all right in his way, you know," he confided in the Colonel, one man to another on a matter of business. "But a bit stick in the mud, if you take my meaning, sir. A bit old *fashioned*, like. Chocolate, caramel and toffee, that's as far as he took things. But this new, young chap, well, different kettle of fish altogether. *Very* up to the minute, he is"

"A bit of a young thruster, eh?" the Colonel, a hunting man, suggested.

"Oh, very go-ahead, sir," Mr Pugh agreed. "Very modern – moves with the times, you know? Something I sometimes think we could do with a bit of round here," he added and chuckled, as if not really meaning it, while thinking of the Imperial Stores in Kingham, with the tills ringing like Christmas, and the girls sitting at them in short, tight nylon coats, brazenly made-up and showing all they've got, before coming back to Miss Wyndham and her fudge.

Mr Pugh's own, khaki shop coat was buttoned all the way up, the breast pocket bristling with Biros. He removed one delicately, like an instrument, and turning to a row of large glass jars on the bottom shelf behind him tapped smartly on several of them in turn.

"Clotted cream fudge with double chocolate," he announced. "*Double* chocolate." The pen tapped again. "Vanilla with chocolate, *and* Vanilla with meringue and marshmallow," he said, emphasising the sheer variety involved. "Cherry fudge with chocolate flake. Rum and raisin fudge. And coffee with chocolate," he finished, and waited with a small complacent smirk for her order.

Miss Wyndham lifted a pair of reading glasses hanging on a cord from the pie-crust collar of her blouse, and peered through them at the line of newcomers. The colonel smiled vague encouragement at her.

She wavered, tempted for a moment by the new and exotic.

Before standing firm out of loyalty to a plain, old favourite. "No, thank you, Mr Pugh," she said. "It's very good of you to have gone to all that trouble. But if you don't mind, I think I'll stay with my usual for now."

Mr Pugh glanced at the Colonel, as if sharing with him the sort of thing he had to put up with, and then inclined his head.

"Madam knows best, I'm sure," he said, and showed his teeth again. And then sniffed, sharply, as if at his own hypocrisy. Mr Pugh's head when it came to business was English, but when it came to the English his heart was Welsh, and unruly.

The shopkeeper, sucking on a tooth, keeping his thoughts to himself, shook the fudge out onto the scales, a notice sitting in front of it informing his customers that, '*A False Measure Is An Abomination To The Lord. But A Just Weight Is His Delight*'.

"I'm on my way to visit Mrs Tranter. She hasn't been well lately." Miss Wyndham blurted it out to the Colonel with small agitated movements of her head, in the grip of an inner turbulence over the deception, jowls shaking and frowning up at him as if the untruth were his.

She paid for her sweets, her glance lingering briefly on the new jar of clotted cream and double chocolate. She could always, she told herself, drop in again tomorrow.

She glanced back with narrowed eyes at the Colonel before closing the door, quietly, behind her.

"Lady orchid. *Orchis purpurea,*" she breathed, Mata Hari of the wildflowers.

Chapter Eleven

Miss Wyndham made sure no one was looking before unwrapping one of her treats outside the shop. She put the rest with her purse in the wicker basket of the bicycle, which was already stuffed with a cardigan, her field guide to wildflowers, last month's copy of the parish magazine, *The Batch Valley Voice*, the Polo mints, sugar cubes and the few carrots she always carried for any horses she might meet, a string bag containing her camera, sketch pad, pencil case and magnifying glass, one tin of cat food overlooked from yesterday's shopping, the book on British hangmen she kept forgetting to return to Phineas Cook, and, even though the sky was blameless of rain clouds, a black sou'wester, just in case.

She did not, of course, hold with eating in the street. But she told herself that she could always stop sucking if she met someone, as she followed the river along the High Street, past the turning on the left for Upper Ham and the Masters' Cottages and Mrs Tranter, with only the briefest of glances in that direction.

Love and war, as far as Miss Wyndham was concerned, were not the only things all was fair in. There was also amateur botany, and Colonel Ash.

The Colonel was her rival in that pursuit and she had been determined to steal a march on him in time for next month's meeting of the Batch Magna Flora and Fauna Society. And early yesterday evening, while on yet another field expedition in Cutterbach, the wood above the village, and about to call it a day, she had stumbled on the means to do so, a single flower, growing there as if waiting for her to find it.

On her knees among the midges and summer grasses in one of the glades, she had peered with mounting excitement at what she had been sure was a lady orchid, its head of crowded delicate pink flowers standing alone among the dark purple of a clump of fly orchids.

Lady orchid, *orchis purpurea*, her field book confirmed it. And further told her that it was locally common in a few sites in Kent and very rare in locations elsewhere. Very rare, very *rare*, she told herself, peddling home with her secret.

And now she was on her way back there with a camera *and* a sketchbook, just in case.

Sucking on the last of the fudge, Miss Wyndham left the village, and turned right past Batch Hall into the lane called Roman Bank, labouring up it as far as her legs and breath would take her. And then dismounting to walk the rest of the way, up one of the hills of the valley that, in more frivolous mood, she sometimes pushed her bike up simply in order to free-wheel down.

Not that there'd be any of that sort of thing this morning. This morning, Miss Wyndham had one thing only on her mind, was intent on it, puffing and blowing over the handlebars, pushing on up to Cutterbach Wood.

Chapter Twelve

She followed the lane which twisted round the top of the hill to the ancient stretch of woodland, the flowers which grew there with the orchids, such as yellow archangel, enchanter's nightshade and dog's mercury, telling of its medieval past.

She dismounted again and walked her bicycle along one of the rides, leaving the sunshine behind, a few stray notes of birdsong loud in the ancient dimness of the wood, deepening the silences there.

She was concentrating on looking for the arrangement of several stones she'd placed one side of the ride before leaving yesterday, a sign indicating the game trail leading off it to the orchid glade. A secret sign, as she, secretly, thought of it, while at the same time having nothing to do with such foolishness. There were times when Miss Wyndham could become quite exasperated with herself.

She found the stones, and leaving her bike there took the path to where the confounding of Colonel Ash and the talk of next month's meeting of the Flora and Fauna Society waited for her undisturbed. She set about the business of recording it, first on film and then on paper, with footnotes detailing time, date and weather conditions, and when she couldn't think of anything to put down, made her way back to her bicycle with the evidence.

She heard them first, when about to leave, the string bag tucked away safely in her basket. And then she spotted them, through the trees. They were walking parallel to the ride but some distance from her and further back. And Miss Wyndham, that part of Miss Wyndham which dealt in secret signs, carefully laid her bicycle down again.

She slipped behind the concealing trunk of an English oak on the edge of the ride, and peering round it lowered her bloodhound gaze in their direction

She counted four of them, four men, none of whom she recognised, carrying guns, and they had dogs with them. Poachers. On their wretched way, she had no doubt, to the pheasant coverts, for the birds Sion Owen was bringing on for the season in October, and the first shoot on the estate for paying guns. Doing his bit not only for the estate but, as she saw it, for Batch Magna.

For Miss Wyndham, who, apart from a spell of war work in Liverpool, had never known anywhere else but Batch Magna, and for whom the estate had always been there, the two come more or less to the same thing.

And now four miscreants, four *outsiders*, were brazenly strolling in to reap the benefit, to steal the fruits of other people's labour.

Miss Wyndham's view of life had a robust simplicity to it. There were those who worked and those who didn't. Those who put in and those who took out. And it made her mad.

She had no idea what she intended doing about it – had no idea what she *could* do, which didn't, of course, stop her trying to do it.

She started up the game trail determined to cut them off.

She was almost there, almost at the spot where their paths would meet, when she realised that she had made a mistake. Watching their approach through the trees she saw that they weren't poachers. They were much worse than that, much worse than simply thieves. That they weren't carrying guns, but spades.

"*Baiters*!" she whispered fiercely, their voices excited and cruel on the summer air as they drew nearer.

On their way to dig out a fox or badger. And she knew what for, knew what would happen then. She had seen the torn and bloody evidence their dogs had left behind.

Miss Wyndham's body shook with anger and her hands closed on an image of her late father's 12 bore she kept on the wall above the Rayburn, and the cartridges in their bright red boxes in a drawer of the kitchen dresser. And she could shoot too, her father had made sure of that. She could quite easily bag all four of them. The two carrying the spades first, and then a quick reload for the other pair, on the wing as it were, in full flight by then no doubt, running for their skins. The Cowards!

But there was no 12 bore, only an old lady, on her own and flustered suddenly with fear. Because people who took pleasure in the torture and drawn-out death of animals would not, she was in no doubt, hesitate to dispose of an eyewitness.

Miss Wyndham knew about murder. She had spent many a contented hour with Phineas Cook disinterring their favourite cases, their conversation littered with untraceable poisons and blunt instruments, and dismembered parts wrapped in newspaper, like fish, bodies stuffed under floorboards and ominously leaking trunks in left-luggage offices.

And now it was her turn, she thought with a certain shocked relish, her hand flying to her mouth.

They'd probably batter her with the spades first, and finish off with their knives. They all carried knives, she'd seen the evidence of that as well. A savage, merciless attack on a defenceless old lady, she thought, as if reading about it. Her blood staining the summer green, silencing the birdsong, the dogs becoming increasingly excited as her killers made sure the old trout was well and truly done for.

And then they'd bury her in a lonely shallow grave, and chuck her bicycle into the river.

Miss Wyndham shut her eyes, as she used to as a child, when unnamed horrors waited on the landing and breathed in the creaking, bedtime dark, hiding from them behind closed lids. Shut her eyes tight and waited to take her place in the annals of bloody murder.

And when she opened them again she saw that they were no longer there, or no longer heading straight for her.

They had veered off before reaching her and obviously hadn't seen her. They were walking at an oblique angle from her, and in single file and silently now, intent.

And she opened her mouth as if to shout, and even, for a dithering moment, thought of running after them.

Because she knew then where they were heading.

She had been there herself only yesterday afternoon, before coming across the orchid, taking a present of a bag of peanuts to the badgers and the cubs they'd had in March. She had scattered the nuts and waited, knowing they'd have picked up the movements above, watching from cover as first the two adults appeared, purblind and snuffling, their rubbery noses questing the air, followed trustingly by their litter of three cubs.

That's where the baiters were heading, for the sett in the blackthorn thicket. They were after the badgers and their young.

"*I must get help! I must get help!*" she kept telling herself, muttering and glancing round fearfully at them now and then as she hurried back down to the ride to do so, clutching her heart when a wood pigeon volleyed out of a sallow bush as she passed, and frantically flapping a hand, shushing a wren, scolding her from the top of an oak, to silence.

She half ran with her bicycle, bouncing it over the rutted and horseshoe-punched ride, and when out of the wood peddled furiously, head down, back along the lane as if getting up speed for the hill, as if for flight, and then, lifting off, free-wheeled down it.

The wind tore the hat with the jay's feather in it from her head, and tugged hanks of her hair loose, and lifted the thick

cabbage-green skirt as she flew grimly on. She remembered at
the last minute, when it would have been too late anyway, to
test the brakes, and was relieved to find that she *had* fitted the
new brake blocks after all, urgently ringing her bell at nothing
as, leaning dangerously to one side, she swept round into the
lane for the Hall.

Chapter Thirteen

The flagged cavernous kitchen of Batch Hall echoed with the barking of the Hall's three dogs and the shrieking of Jasmine's twins attempting to ride a couple of them.

Until Sarah, a cousin of Humphrey's, shut them up with a sudden, piercing yelp that got everyone's attention.

"You tell 'em, Sarah," Sion said.

"It always works with my dogs," Sarah said mildly, and went back to the cigarette she was rolling.

Jasmine dealt with the twins. "Sit back there, the both of you. Before I lamp you! Showing me up like that. And drink the squash Mrs Owen was good enough to get you."

Jasmine had dropped in for coffee, bringing the twins and her youngest with her, leaving her oldest daughter, Meredith, in charge of the rest. The twins went back to their straws and the squash at the table, where Jasmine's youngest daughter, sucking noisily on a Welsh heart, was sitting on Humphrey's lap in an island of calm having a story read to her.

He and Clem had returned from their honeymoon a fortnight ago, and having, as he thought of it, made a start on their own family, he was now getting some practice in.

The twins had interrupted their mother as she was about to play one of the two fruit machines in the kitchen, waiting with a sort of studied casualness to take Phineas's place at it. Jasmine had a plan.

Phineas also had a sort of plan when he played the slots, as Humphrey called them, bringing a touch of Vegas into a Batch Magna kitchen, one rather less logical than Jasmine's.

On his last gamble, he would always walk away immediately after spinning the reels, as if indifferent to the result.

He was waiting for luck to astonish him, waiting for it to strike when he wasn't looking, the way he'd seen it happen in a film once. Waiting for a fabled year's worth of jackpots to arrive at once in a cascade of coins, and then, gasping with surprised delight, filling his pockets and stuffing them down his shirt front and into his Panama hat.

And Jasmine's plan was to wait until Phineas or Shelly, or whoever was playing at the time, had shortened the odds she'd read about somewhere, and then to step in and collect the jackpot that had only just been missed.

It didn't work this time either. But given the shortening odds, the way Jasmine calculated it, ignoring the times she wasn't there to witness them shortening perhaps in someone else's favour, it was only a matter of time.

Phineas, poorer than when he came in, had gone back to his coffee and the gossipy company of Annie and Priny. Clem and her mother-in-law had left for the discount shop in Penycwn, leaving Annie in charge. Priny had also dropped in for coffee, and Phineas, taking time off from his typewriter, had arrived hotfooted with news that obviously couldn't be entrusted to the telephone.

They had, he'd been pleased to report, beaming round at the company, their first customers for the punt on the river business. A young couple, seeing the ad in one of the local papers, couldn't *wait* to sign on for it – which hadn't in the least surprised him, as he himself was the author of the advertisement.

It was, he considered, if he did say so himself, a masterpiece of enticement.

It read:

MEMORIES ARE MADE OF THIS

A romantic evening trip on a punt for two (crewed by a fully trained and experienced punter). Enjoy the magic of the peaceful River Cluny under the stars and the weeping willows. Make memories together while sipping wine (a bottle of fine wine is included in the price) by the light of coloured lanterns.

Book early to avoid disappointment

He'd got the idea of the lanterns from old Tom Parr, who used to work as an engineer and fireman for the Cluny Steamboat Company, and who had told him about the Moonlight Excursions the company used to run in the summer, with coloured lanterns on deck and courting couples in the shadows. Phineas had been immediately taken by the idea.

He hadn't actually got any coloured lanterns, but he had borrowed a couple of old hurricane lamps from Owain. They'd last been used when Owain was keepering, and one of them was a bit on the smoky side after all this time. But Phineas took the view that any couple intent on making memories under the stars, and all that, wouldn't take an awful lot of notice of the details.

Sarah was sitting at the other end of the table with Sion. Sarah farmed at Cuckington, near Kingham, with her husband, John, but when younger had run the estate office in the days when there was still something left to run, and was now acting on an ad hoc basis as estate manager.

She had arranged to meet Sion to discuss the autumn pheasant shoot. Owain's son from a first marriage was now the estate's gamekeeper. Sion, who as a toddler had often been lugged about by his father in a grain sack when Owain was working in the woods, and who had been given his first gun, a little .410, when he was eleven, had been born in the estate's Keeper's Cottage. And now, after the death of an estate pensioner that winter, was back there, and once again there were working dogs in the kennels at the back and ferrets in the hutches.

The job was part time and, apart from a dog allowance, unpaid, but the cottage, as it had done in his father's day, came rent and rates free. And when Sion wasn't keepering for the estate, he was out doing a bit on neighbouring estates, at night, filling backdoor orders for local hotels, pubs and restaurants, his .22 rifle, with its short cartridges, no louder in the darkness of the woods than a sheep's fart, as he put it. And when he wasn't at that, he was working as a terrierman for the hunt, or as a woodsman, with a sideline in fire logs, or as a stock fencer, or tree trimmer, or anything else he could lend a strong arm and a Ford pick-up truck to.

Sarah had moved on to other estate shoots, before the war, "The general ran them purely as a hobby then, as he did the fishing, for himself and friends. The estate was farmed for shooting. The tenants paid ridiculously low rents, but they had to grow what the head keeper told them to grow, and to keep something like six yards of grass headlands for the partridge. Well, you know how small the fields are here. The only one surprised when the estate finally went bust was the general. He was a dear old thing, the dearest. But he had *absolutely* no head for business."

"And here's to him," Sion said, lifting his coffee mug.

"Yes," Sarah agreed, "here's to him."

She flipped a Zippo lighter at a roll-up she'd been making.

"And everything had to be done properly, down to the head keeper's suits – and this was before Owain's time in the job, of course. There was a seasonal lightweight cloth of lovat green for partridge mornings, and a thicker, dark green suit on pheasant

76

days, both topped with a brown bowler, with a gold ribbon and two gold braid acorns on it. The head keeper we had then, when I was a young girl, used to wear his at a rakish angle. *Very* dashing, he looked. William, his name was. William Boyce ..."

Sarah's voice had drifted off and her cigarette had gone out.

"He had those quite *brilliant* blue eyes – and such a wicked twinkle," she went on, while Sion shifted in his chair and wondered what he was listening to.

"All the women fancied him like stink, including me, I have to say. I had the most *terrific* pash on him. Well, as I say, I was young. Just eighteen ..."

Sion glanced round, as if looking for support, or escape. Sarah, who seemed to have been talking to herself, relit her roll-up and coolly blew out smoke.

"He had a rearing hut up in the coverts, and, of course, he could be there all night sometimes. It had a stove and a few sticks of furniture, and a bed, a camp bed, in it. Well, you can imagine the rumours that used to fly about the village. Talk about Lady Chatterley's Lover, and the rough kiss of a blanket, and all that," she added, and made a humorous face.

Sion took his cue from that and laughed politely.

He didn't know what was worse, Sarah going on like some young bird or Sarah making one of those unfunny, boring jokes that old people make. And it had to be a joke, this was Sarah. A grey-haired granny in brown bib overalls and a man's shirt, and with dirt embedded in her cracked fingernails. And he had never known her to look any different. Frosty Sarah, with her jolly hockey sticks accent and a tongue when crossed like a triffid, as Phineas had put it.

Sarah laughed with him, as if finding the idea that she could ever have been involved in anything like that as amusingly preposterous as he seemed to.

But the real amusement was in her eyes, the memory of who she had once been, if only for a short while, before toeing the line she was expected to toe. Her world for fifty years had been her husband and family, and the farm, and her dogs and horses, and doing her duty on various charity committees, and on the Bench. And she had long regarded what had really gone on back then, the rest of the story from that time, to be nobody's business but hers.

"In those days," she went on, that part of her past locked away again, "the guns would shoot pheasant and partridge up until luncheon, and then move down to the river."

"For the duck shoot," Sion said. "Something we ought to look at again, Sarah."

She nodded. "Yes, just what I had in mind."

"Wouldn't do as well as the pheasant, like, or when we get round to it, the partridge. But we'd still come out of it with a few bob, surely?"

"I'm sure of it. But it would need to be managed, of course. For some reason there were far more about then. Especially when it was really cold. The Cluny used to be covered with them, widgeon and teal, and snipe on the water meadows, as thick as starlings sometimes."

"Now, that would give 'em a good bit of sport, the old snipe. And we could tie it in with –" Whatever Sion was about to suggest they tie it in with was cut short by another outbreak of barking, until the dogs recognised the visitor.

Miss Wyndham, red-faced, dishevelled and hatless, stood clutching at her heart in the doorway, catching her breath as if the next one might be her last.

"Hattie," Sarah said quietly into the startled silence.

Sarah never fussed, never panicked, and unless in competition with her dogs, never usually raised her voice. She never usually had to.

She got up and led Miss Wyndham to a chair, and the others gathered round her while Miss Wyndham sat, chest heaving, blowing at tendrils of escaped hair.

Sarah suggested a glass of water. Phineas suggested brandy.

"Except there isn't any," he went on. "There's gin though. Still some left from the welcome home bottle of Plymouth that Priny here and the Commander gave you," he said to Humphrey, more familiar with the Hall's drinks cupboard than he was. "That and two litres of Valpolicella."

"Mom gets them from the discount store," Humphrey told the others.

"Plus some sort of ghastly bilious-green liqueur stuff," Phineas added, making a face.

Miss Wyndham was waving an impatient hand.

"*Baiters*!" she got out then, her breath struggling with the word.

She looked wildly up at them.

"Baiters," she said more distinctly. "They're after the badgers. On their way to kill them. And their cubs."

Jasmine, mindful of the children, swore in Welsh, spitting it out.

"The brutes!" Annie said.

"Where, Hattie?" Sarah asked calmly.

"Cutterbach Wood." She looked at Sion. "The big black-thorn thicket."

Sion nodded. "I know."

"They've got spades. And guns." Miss Wyndham said, confused.

"The coverts are up near there. They're after the bloody pheasants as well," Sion said, indignantly calling the kettle black. "*And* I've got turkeys round there."

The turkeys had been Owain's idea, from a time when food was rationed. They were living wild, fattening up nicely for Christmas on beechnuts, goose grass, stinging nettles and onions. And at night they roosted in the big beeches, lining the lower branches like vultures.

Sion started for the door. "I'll get up there."

"Sion! Best not to," Annie said. "Call the police, there's a love."

"Yes, that's the best thing, Sion," Priny said in support. "Let them deal with it."

Sion looked startled. "The police! What you want to call them for?"

"Well, it's illegal, isn't it?" Priny said.

"Well, yes, it's illegal all right," Sion said, as if wondering what that had to do with it. "But we don't want the coppers in here, poking their noses into everything." There was the out-of-date tax disk on the Ford, for one thing, and a roe buck waiting to be skinned and butchered in the cottage kitchen for another.

"Anyway, by the time that lot get here, those blokes would have long scarpered. No, I'll just nip up there myself, see what's what, like."

"But they've got guns!" Annie said.

"It's *spades*. They've got spades. Just spades. Not guns," Miss Wyndham said suddenly. "I remember now. They were carrying spades, spades which I thought at first were guns." She looked agitated, almost tearful. "I'm so sorry ..."

Annie bent down and gave her a hug.

"Hush now, Hattie."

"I won't be long," Sion said.

"Si," Humphrey said, "I'll come with you. It's my land they're doing it on," he added when Sion hesitated. "And I like badgers."

Brock is everyone's favourite uncle in the woods, the Commander had told him. A bit erratic at times, liable to fly off in all sorts of bad-tempered directions, but a loyal and stout-hearted animal. A bit of a rough diamond, it's true, a bit short of the social graces – but *always* there when needed.

"And I'll come as well," Sarah put in. "As witness."

Phineas stepped forward.

80

"No, Sarah. *I* will go," he said, offering himself. "This is men's work. Women are for weeping."

"Now, hold on a minute," Sion put in. "Phin, I think it's best if you stayed here. Be more official like, with just the two of us. The landowner and his gamekeeper, see."

Phineas agreed immediately.

"Yes, yes, I quite see that. Well, if you're absolutely sure …?"

"I still think you should leave it to the police," Annie said fretfully.

Her stepson smiled at her.

"Look, darling – look, all we're going to do is to get the number of whatever they've got parked up there. Then we can call the police, when we've got something to give them, see, something for them to go on. All right?"

But Annie wasn't buying it, wasn't buying that smile; she'd spent too many years with his father for that.

"You just take care, Sion, that's all," she said gravely.

"Just take care. Both of you. And get your haircut," she added as they were leaving, another way of telling him to take care.

Sitting in the cab of Sion's pick-up on the way down the drive, Humphrey asked what baiters actually *did* to the animals. Sion told him.

Humphrey spent the rest of the journey staring rigidly ahead, his face under his baseball cap set and determined-looking.

Chapter Fourteen

They found the vehicle, a white 20-cwt van, some way past the ride into the wood Miss Wyndham had taken, parked up round a bend in the lane.

A scribbled note stuck behind one of the windscreen wipers said that the driver had broken down and had gone for help. The van doors were locked.

Sion jotted down the van's number on the back of a betting slip.

"Right," he said, "well, we've got their number."

Humphrey nodded. "Yeah."

"And there'll be plenty of evidence left."

"Yeah ..." Humphrey said again, neither man making a move back to the Ford.

The sound of a distant tractor reached them on the still air, from one of the fields below maybe, or working on the slopes on the other side of the valley, and there was a woodpecker somewhere, hammering away in bursts.

And then their heads went up at the sudden clamour of dogs. At least two of them, deep in the wood. And then silence.

"Could mean they're still digging," Sion said quietly. "The dogs still waiting to get to work, and getting impatient about it. Either that or ..." He shrugged.

Humphrey's imagination, fuelled by what Sion had told him on the way there, filled in the rest.

"To hell with it – come on!" he said suddenly, jerking his head at the wood.

Sion, looking unsurprised, laughed. "You sure now, Humph?"

Humphrey, his mouth clamped shut, nodded briefly.

"You're the boss," Sion said.

Sion was shorter than the American but as wide in the shoulders, a compact Welsh bullock in the scrum when he turned out for Bannog Rugby Club, and an enthusiastic veteran of pub brawls either side of the border, which to him, full of Saturday night beer and the sort of energy that had to go *somewhere*, had been just another form of contact sport.

"Hold on a minute, though. No need to be daft about it."

Humphrey followed him to the pick-up. Sion leaned over into the back of the truck, and sorting through his tools came up with a spare shaft for a felling axe and what looked like a shovel with most of the blade missing down its length.

He thought about it and then handed the axe shaft to Humphrey.

"There's a good bit of weight in that, and it's got a nice balance to it. Just in case, like, that's all. I'm more used to this," he added, hoisting the other tool over a shoulder.

Humphrey hefted the polished hickory shaft in a meaty hand, and then gripping it in both hands took a swipe at the air.

"You've done that before, Humph," Sion said, grinning at Humphrey in his prized blue and red baseball cap.

Humphrey stuck his jaw out. "Yeah, well, I used to be a batter with the South Bronx Renegades. Not league stuff or anything," he added modestly, remembering that he wasn't supposed to make things up any more. "Just kids, y'know? A gang from the neighbourhood? Broke a few windows in my time, though. What's that you've got, Si?" he asked chummily.

"It's a graft, what's called a grafter spade. Useful for digging holes for fence posts, and for rabbiting. I use it for both. It's handy for digging down for a ferret when it's gone to sleep, or has stopped to eat what it's supposed to drive out."

"Do you know where these guys are?" Humphrey asked then.

Sion couldn't decide whether the American was nervous or simply eager to get going.

"Yeah. I know where they are. We'll go in their way, have a look see if we can find where they went in. We'll try up the lane first. Poachers always go *up* from whatever they've arrived in. Don't ask me why." He did it himself, and still didn't understand it.

They walked back past the white van. The strands of barbed-wire fencing along that stretch of the lane were rusting but still in place, the posts still upright.

"There's not much of that left, I can tell you," Sion said, nodding at the wire.

"Yeah. We'll have to get something done about it, when we've got some spare bread," Humphrey said automatically, words said countless times since taking on the estate. "And maybe put up a notice board or something," he added vaguely.

They heard the dogs again, as they carried on up the lane, the sound rearing and then dying. On one of the fields opposite, fenced with tall summer hedgerows, a few large Friesians were gazing up against the five-barred gate. They lurched away in a confused scramble when they walked past, cattle and men catching each other by surprise.

Humphrey's heart jumped. Sion merely glanced at them. He was still humming away quietly to himself, grafter on one shoulder, a man on his way to nothing more fraught than a spot of rabbiting.

"This is it," he said then. "This is where they went in."

A path had been made by feet crossing a nettle bed running along the verge. On the bank above it the fencing had collapsed, the wire strands part buried under earth and dead leaves.

They went in the same way, using the bough of a hawthorn bush as a handhold to clamber up the bank.

Sion pointed out the path the baiters had taken. Above them a thrush paused abruptly in its song, as if stopping to listen, and then opened again, a shower of notes falling in the green gloom as they moved through the trees. Ahead of them the clamour of the dogs rose again briefly and then fell, leaving behind a deeper silence.

"Now, we're going to do this all legal, like, Humph. Right?" Sion said in a low voice.

"Yeah. Yeah, sure, Si," Humphrey said distractedly. He was busy wondering if the dogs were tied up.

"We'll identify ourselves, and ask them to leave. We'll confiscate their gear – we're allowed to do that – tell them we've got their van number and that we'll be reporting them to the police. We can only use violence to protect ourselves. That's the law," Sion added sternly, rather enjoying the novelty of being on the right side of it for once. "Okay?"

"Okay," Humphrey nodded.

Sion looked at him and laughed.

"You'd better get behind me, they'll see you coming a mile off. Think there's a forest fire, they will," he said, more a reference to Humphrey's shirt than his cap, the violent clash of reds and greens on it.

Humphrey lumbered on behind him, Sion glancing back sharply now and then as another dry stick snapped. Sion himself moved soundlessly, a gift inherited from his father, who could still get within ten feet of a deer without the animal knowing it.

They heard their voices first, as Miss Wyndham had done, nearing the thicket glade.

And then they saw them.

Humphrey followed Sion from the cover of one tree to another, walking on tiptoe now, mouth open in concentration, as if about to jokingly surprise someone.

Some fifteen or twenty yards away from the baiters, the two men watched from behind the wide shelter of a beech, the sun filtering peacefully through the new green of its leaves.

They were still digging. There were four of them. One man was working on the bank below the blackthorns, not much more than his head visible, throwing up spadefuls of red earth, another was leaning on his spade, taking a break.

There were two dogs, both tied up, Humphrey was relieved to see. They were straining at the end of their tethers, eyes fixed on the deepening hole in the bank, on their bellies one moment, up the next, restless with excitement, and barking again then, until quietened with a flick of the hand from one of the other baiters.

He went across to them and checked one of the ring-ended tethering spikes driven into the ground, testing it with a boot to see if it had loosened.

"He's a strong little bugger. Just look at that chest on him," he said of the dog, which looked to Sion like a bull terrier-Jack Russell cross.

"Yeah, like I said, he cost a good few bob but he's well worth it. Got teeth like a can opener. Have a go at anything, he will. Rip up a dog fox on his own, *no* problem. Took a great boar out last weekend, over at Presteigne. Loves it, he does. They work well together, as you'll see."

One of the others laughed hungrily at the prospect.

"Hey, Jace!" he called. "How are we doing? We're all waiting here!"

"Any minute now," the digger said. "I'm almost through."

"And then it's *play*time," the baiter leaning on the spade said, grinning.

Humphrey was staring at the tethering rings.

A dog drags the badgers out by the head, Sion had told him. The baiters stun them with a spade or whatever, and then stab them, usually in the buttocks – they don't want to kill them too soon – which adds to the smell of blood and excitement in the air. And then they throw them to the dogs.

But sometimes they torture them. Sometimes they skewer their necks with the corkscrew end of a tethering spike and twist. And they keep on twisting, cutting off the animal's screams, and trapping fur and flesh, slowly choking it to death. Brock, everyone's favourite uncle in the woods, a loyal and stout-hearted fellow, always there when needed.

Sion was at that moment about to step forward and do what they'd agreed to do, when Humphrey shot out ahead of him.

Humphrey wasn't much on thinking at the best of times, and he didn't think at all now. He saw an image of the badger's slow torture, saw its paws paddling in the air as if running away, as if escaping in its mind from the pain and terror, and Humphrey just did.

He ran at them. His roar trumpeting through the wood, a baby elephant in a Hawaiian shirt charging out of the bush, followed a startled moment later by Sion, a Welsh bullock, bellowing with him.

The baiter leaning on the spade was the first to recover, violence a reflex with him. His thin trap of a mouth opened in a snarl and he drew back the spade.

Humphrey went straight for him.

He swung the axe shaft, missed the raised trenching tool and got the baiter's hand, and almost in the same movement walloped him across his knee. Humphrey was *very* angry.

The man drew in a deep gulp of air, and went down, screaming as if on fire, while Sion rushed a second, unarmed, baiter, dropping his grafter and using his fists in an exchange of punches, and then wrestling with him.

The dogs were dancing at the end of their tethers, up on their hind legs, spittle flying, the sounds they were making snarled up in their throats, and Humphrey had time to hope that the tethers would hold before being hit hard in his face by the dog man, losing the axe shaft and his baseball cap.

He tried to defend himself against the attack with a flurry of ineffectual, panicky punches, before remembering how he was supposed to be doing it. How, on many a Saturday morning in the Bronx, sitting raptly with a bag of popcorn in the gun-loud dark of a neighbourhood movie theatre, he had watched his childhood hero John Wayne doing it.

He pulled back his right hand and brought it up, a punch with absolutely no skill in it but plenty of meat. Humphrey had never hit anyone on the jaw or anywhere else before, not even in the playground. But he knew immediately he made contact, knew instinctively, that he had knocked the man out, that the baiter was at home one instant, out the next, slumping, a dead weight, at his feet.

Sion was still busy, and Humphrey danced about, fists and his dander up, looking for the fourth man, the digger, and shouting, "*Come on! Come on!*" a different Humphrey from the one who had rather nervously followed Sion into the wood. This Humphrey had already put one man out of business and had now knocked out another.

He wondered if the digger was hiding in his hole, and then he saw him.

He was kneeling, bare chested and mud smeared, by the tethering spikes. The dogs' leashes had been run through the rings and then tied together and he was fumbling with the knots, trying to untie them, but the dogs, in anticipation of being given their heads, were pulling even harder at their leashes, tightening them.

Humphrey ran at him and the man dashed back to the bank under the blackthorns. Humphrey changed course, reaching the hole as the man leaned down and grabbed his spade. All Humphrey could do then was duck.

The trenching spade, swung with the narrow blade flat, passed no more than an inch from his skull, its passage a playful breeze through his hair. Humphrey charged head down from the same position, and toppled the man over the mound of earth and into the hole.

He hauled him out by the legs, his eyes bright with battle, and they rolled over the piled red earth, the man trying to get away, Humphrey trying to hold him there.

But the digger's skin was sleek with mud and sweat. He slipped out of Humphrey's grasp, and jumping to his feet took off through the trees.

Humphrey gamely thought about it, but knew he had no chance of catching him.

Sion's man, the biggest of the four, had shown rather more fight. But Sion had him where he wanted him now, up close, hugging him like a lover, as Owain had taught him, with one foot on his instep to keep him there. And then ramming his head up into his face.

He let him go and the baiter sat abruptly down with a muffled cry, blood seeping through the hands he'd clasped to a broken nose.

Sion swung round, ready for whatever came next. And saw only Humphrey still standing, Humphrey walking up to him with a new-found swagger, dusting dirt off his baseball cap and chewing as if on gum.

"All right, Si?" he asked casually.

Sion, sniffing and getting his breath back, nodded.

He looked at the man groaning on the ground. "Perhaps that will teach you to go attacking innocent people," he said, getting their story in. "Perhaps you'll be reasonable now, and listen. As I said when I identified us, this here is Sir Humphrey Strange, the owner of these woods, and I'm his head keeper," he went on, promoting himself on the spot, while the baiter mumbled something behind his hands.

Sion looked across at the one who had run into the batter from the South Bronx Renegades, curled up, whimpering with pain, holding his wounded hand up and clutching his knee with the other, and at the dog man who was just starting to come round with a 'where am I?' expression, and laughed. Even the dogs looked defeated, down on their bellies, watching them warily.

"Remind me not to argue with you, Humph, next time I argue with you," he said.

Humphrey almost burst with it, nursing the knuckles of his right hand and chewing even harder on nothing.

"Where's the fourth bloke gone?"Sion grinned. "Not still down his hole, is he?"

Humphrey spread his hands. "He ran off. Left his T-shirt behind."

"In a bit of a hurry, was he? Can't say I blame him, neither," Sion said, heaping more pleasure on Humphrey.

He fetched the black T-shirt left on the bank above the hole and tossed it to the baiter nursing his nose on the ground. "Use this. Your mate left it, the one that was in the hole. He did a runner on you. Has he got the van keys?"

The baiter shook his head carefully. Sion then wanted to know if the man had a knife, and when he hesitated Sion asked him again, while prodding him in the chest with a foot. The baiter nodded this time.

They took a lock-knife off each of the three men and added them to the trenching spades.

"We'll keep these as evidence. We've got your van number and we'll be reporting this to the police. Now take your dogs and clear off."

"And the next time we see you guys round here it'll be the last time for you – know whadda I mean?" Humphrey said, and chewed on nothing again. Give him a black shirt, a white tie and a Tommy gun, Sion thought, and he'd go and see him any day at the Kingham Odeon.

"Now beat it," Humphrey snarled.

They watched them leave, the baiter Humphrey had walloped on the knee hopping along on one leg, leaning on the shoulder of his mate, who had the T-shirt pressed to his nose. The dog man's expression, as he pulled up the tethering spikes and trailed after them with his dogs, suggested that whatever the picture was at the moment he still wasn't altogether in it.

They saved their grins until the three had disappeared into the trees.

"You'll have a right shiner in the morning, Humph," Sion said then.

"And you," Humphrey said.

"Yeah. Must be getting old, letting him catch me like that." Sion's grin spread. "Good though, wasn't it?"

"Yeah. It *was* good, Si, wasn't it?" Humphrey agreed.

"Right then, well," Sion said, "we'll put Brock's front door back for him before we go, shall we?"

Chapter Fifteen

Nearly a fortnight after the Battle of Cutterbach Wood, as it had become known, Miss Wyndham rode again past the Hall and turned right into Roman Bank, and once more dismounted to push her bicycle up the hill.

Past Frog Leasow, Padford, Sallow, Perry, Snails Park and Hollow Oak, she knew all the old field names and what grew where and when. And unlike the last outing to Cutterbach Wood, felt relaxed enough to enjoy it all now, now that the find of the lady orchid was safely in the bag, as she had learned to say since the arrival of Sir Humphrey.

The rain that had lashed the valley, falling almost without let up for over a week, had stopped and the sun was back, the air scented with the earth drying under it, and summer in the hedgerows. The leaves of the two big copper beeches on Snails Park were wine dark now, the hedge hawthorns bowed under falls of blossom like snow, and swallows skimmed low over the green and gold painted fields, feeding on the wing.

Halfway up, on a meadow smelling of rabbits, a chestnut hunter was out with a few sooty brown-black sheep and a donkey companion, grazing, tail swishing, on the freshened succulent grass, its coat polished amber in the sun.

Miss Wyndham rattled the iron field gate.

The hunter looked up and then snootily ignored her, but the donkey trotted over in an amiable, untidy sort of way, and bared its teeth at her like Mr Pugh.

She asked it how it was first, following Jasmine Roberts's example when it came to meeting animals. Miss Wyndham wasn't entirely convinced that they did understand, but in case they did it would be a breach of good manners not to say *something*. She commented on the other animal's rudeness, and told the donkey that, just for that, it could have the horse's share of the treats as well.

The donkey bared its teeth again at the news, and she fed it two carrots, followed by four mints and the same amount of sugar cubes for, as it were, pudding, and then wiped its slobber off on her skirt.

Miss Wyndham paused at the top of the hill for another breather, dabbing at her neck and face with a lace handkerchief she kept tucked in a sleeve.

Below her all was as it should be, as it had always been, the roofs of the village under the shelter of the tower of St Swithin's, the tall, star-shaped chimneys of Batch Hall above the trees, and the river glimpsed, glittering, through them, the swollen water spitting light.

And Miss Wyndham gazed with satisfaction on the scene, her expression suggesting that that was *exactly* what she meant.

She took a deep breath, the air scented with hawthorn blossom and meadow sweet and honeysuckle. Early summer in the valley, her favourite time of the year.

When, that is, it wasn't the fullness of late summer, the last fling of the year. And *when*, that is, out of fairness to that season, it wasn't spring, she reminded herself, as she peddled on round the lane to the wood, spring breaking out everywhere like buttons popping, as she thought of it. Or autumn, she mustn't forget autumn. Its fire growing more poignant for her each passing year, when the mists above the Cluny lingered on into mornings smelling of apples, and there were spiders' webs in the lanes and field mushrooms for breakfast. And even winter, even when the valley was iron with frosts as hard as a Puritan's heart, as the Commander had put it, and the cold found her bones. Yes, even winter, she told herself firmly, determined to be fair about it, muttering away as she once again dismounted to walk her bicycle along the ride.

She followed the same game trail up from the ride on her way to the badgers, carrying again a gift of peanuts.

She stopped now and then, and looked quickly behind her, her bloodhound gaze sweeping suspiciously through the trees. But she saw no one, and heard only the birds, opening up fully again after the rain, singing to the sun, or scolding and twittering, nesting and feeding.

They hadn't caught the baiters. The number plates on the van turned out to be false. It wasn't even known which police force should investigate it, which side of the border they were from. Not that she seriously expected them to be back, not after the drubbing she'd been delighted to learn they'd received.

Which didn't stop her turning swiftly now and then, as if to surprise someone.

Standing in front of the blackthorn thicket, she saw where the hole had been dug and then filled in again. The loose earth there had dipped under the weight of the rain, putting her in mind of some of her less successful attempts at pastry.

She scattered the nuts, noting with pleasure that there was a fresh jumble of small paw prints in the play area in front of the sett. But she didn't wait, didn't stay this time to watch from cover as the badgers came up to investigate, but hurried back to her bicycle.

Riding back along the lane, she kept telling herself not to be silly, that it was the memory of the baiters in the wood that had unsettled her.

But she couldn't help feeling that a shadow had fallen across the morning, as if the sun had gone in, and stayed in.

A shadow which seemed to follow her from the wood all the way back to the village.

Chapter Sixteen

Phineas couldn't be entirely sure about *everything* that happened that night, during the inaugural trip of the punt on the river business. He'd admitted as much, that the picture as he remembered it lacked clarity in *every* single detail, but what he was sure about, even if others seemed not to be, was that he was not to blame. Not this time. And certainly not altogether.

As he had attempted to explain to Sarah, when up at the Hall the following morning on Captain's Report, as the Commander termed it. He, Phineas, had wide experience of women – he'd married three of them. But when it came to simply refusing to understand things, Sarah was in a class of her own.

He could only feel sorry for the miscreants who appeared before her on the Bench.

She had sat across the table from him in the kitchen, arms folded, just the two of them. Everyone else, no doubt, was still in bed. Where he should be. Where he *had* been, until roused from it by his son, Daniel, who'd taken the phone call from her.

He had half sleepwalked up to the Hall, feeling like something his dog had dug up, with the bells of St Swithin's, clamouring out for Matins, following him as if browbeating him as he trudged off in the opposite direction.

He usually made an effort to attend most Sundays, but not today, even if he'd been allowed to. He didn't feel like being shouted at today.

The Reverend Cutler, normally a perfectly mild-mannered, inoffensive sort of chap, could get quite heated about what was wrong with them all when he was in the pulpit, including the Reverend Cutler. Firing the stuff off with the air of a man who had just received another rocket from head office and who didn't jolly well see why he should have to take all the blame.

And Sarah hadn't even offered him a cup of anything, not even a glass of water.

Right, well, for a start, he told her, the couple who had signed on for the romantic trip for two by coloured lanterns and all the rest of it had been having a tiff before they arrived, that was perfectly obvious. All right, he wasn't actually *there*, on the *Belle*, at the time he'd given them Nor, to be absolutely honest about it, was he there when they *did* arrive. But he had nipped down from the pub at around the time they were *due* to arrive, anyone could tell her that. And he'd left a note which they found when they finally – well, arrived.

Spent by the effort, Phineas tenderly cupped a hand to his brow.

"So you were in the pub?" was all Sarah said.

He lifted haggard eyes to her face, a woman sans merci, and sighed.

"Yes, Sarah," he admitted heavily. "I was in the pub."

"Instead of where you were supposed to be?"

He sighed again. "Yes, Sarah, instead of where I was supp-osed to be."

"Might one ask why?" Sarah enquired mildly. "I mean, while I appreciate, Phineas, that you weren't charging the estate for your services, it nevertheless reflects badly –"

"Ken Hollywell!" Phineas suddenly remembered. "It was Ken Hollywell! He turned up earlier at the *Belle*. With a cigar."

It was all coming back to him now. "His wife gave birth in the afternoon and he invited me to wet the baby's head," he said, offering it to her with a sickly-looking smile, one meant to invite her to find it as sweetly charming as he did. "Ken and Wendy Hollywell. At Upper Reach Farm," he stumbled on when Sarah said nothing, just sat there, looking at him. "A daughter. Yesterday afternoon, at Kingham General. Seven pounds two ounces," he said, as if reading it out of a newspaper, and put a hand again to his brow.

"And then … And then, well, as you know …"

"Yes, Phineas," she agreed, "I do know. Your passengers ended up having to stay there overnight, if only in order to have dry clothes in the morning. Dilly gave them my number earlier and the boyfriend lost no time in using it. But first the good news, which won't take long. Owain and Sion have recovered the punt – Owain's *favourite* fishing punt, he tells me –"

"Favourite? He's only got one."

"Well, as it's Owain's punt, which he generously puts to the estate's use, we must allow him to describe it as he wishes."

Phineas wasn't sure about that. It depended on what it was going to cost him. He could be a crafty old blighter, Owain.

"Be that as it may, he also tells me that, happily, the punt is repairable."

"Oh, good, I was wondering about that," Phineas murmured.

"And at no cost to the estate – Owain said he can do it himself."

"Good old Owain!" Phineas said, shaking his head in admiration, and then wincing as his headache took a swipe at him.

"The six cushions borrowed from the Owens, you'll further be glad to know, were also recovered, along with the pole. Eventually."

Phineas, who'd forgotten about both the cushions and the pole, nodded carefully and said he'd been wondering about those, as well.

"The two storm lanterns were both smashed, but you must make your own settlement with Owain concerning those. And now for the rest of it," Sarah went on relentlessly, looking at a sheet of writing paper in front of her. "As I said, the boyfriend –"

"Adrian, his name is."

"– the boyfriend lost no time in ringing me at home. I made a note of what he had to say. It transpired that he's a lawyer."

The revelation galvanised Phineas.

"A *lawyer*? I might have known – I might have *known*! I don't like to talk behind a man's back, Doctor Johnson said, but I believe the fellow's a lawyer. Let's kill all the lawyers," he muttered fiercely. "Shakespeare knew –"

"A lawyer," Sarah rolled on, "who intends suing the estate for despoiled clothes, presumably meaning wet –"

Phineas looked outraged.

"Now, that *really* wasn't my fault – he was in charge of the punt at the time. He was the one with the pole."

Sarah looked at him. "And where, might one ask, were you?"

"Sitting with Suzanne, his girlfriend." He remembered that all right. It was what made his suffering this morning bearable. It was how he had got there, that was the bit he wasn't at all sure about.

"And how – never mind, Phineas, never mind."

Sarah went back to her sheet of paper.

"Along with the clothes, he is also suing for the loss of a Marks and Spencer cardigan. His girlfriend –"

"Suzanne," Phineas said tenderly.

"– his girlfriend will buy a replacement and send us the bill."

Phineas looked shocked. Was that all he had meant to her?

He had told himself afterwards that, despite the rather damp end to things, they had met and gone on a journey together, when they had steered briefly by the stars before parting forever. His words of farewell, he told himself bitterly now, had been written in his heart. Hers would be a replacement chit for an M&S cardigan.

"He, the boyfriend –"

"Adrian. He likes to be called Adrian," Phineas said sulkily.

Sarah looked up. "Isn't that his real name then?" she asked, alert to possible legal loopholes.

"Well, yeah, I s'pose it is," he muttered.

She thought for a moment of pursuing it, and then gave up. It was easier sometimes getting sense out of a five-year-old than it was out of Phineas Cook.

"Well, anyway, in addition to the clothes he intends suing for personal injuries –"

Phineas sat up. "*What*! Personal injuries? A few cuts and bruises, that's all. And what are *im*personal injuries, that's what I'd like to know."

"For –"

"It's the same when people swank about so and so being *personal* friends of theirs," he went tetchily on. "So what's –"

"For," Sarah cut in, upping the volume, "personal injuries, and distress caused by the hazards they had to endure –"

"Haz–*hazards*!" He looked about him as if for someone to share it with. "What hazards! They got wet, that's all. *I* got wet."

"The cold he tells me he now has, having to tramp back in wet clothes to the village. And the cost of an enforced overnight stay at the Steamer Inn."

Sarah leaned back in her chair.

"And they rather want their money back. Understandable enough I suppose, in the circumstances. I take it you still have the fee?"

"Hmm? Yes, yes, of course," he said, wondering if he'd spent it all in the pub, or if what was left of it had ended up in the river. "I don't happen to have it on me at the moment. I'll drop it in later." When he'd borrowed it from one of the others. All he knew was that there had been nothing in his trousers when he went through them before leaving.

"Now, I've given it some thought," Sarah went on, "and I think it reasonable, Phineas, that you reimburse the dry cleaning, the cost of the cardigan, and their stay at the pub." She waited.

"Yes, yes, all right," he said weakly. He'd have agreed to anything just as long as it meant he could go back to bed.

"Good. Now, as the estate has no intention of handing over whatever this lawyer thinks fit, even if the estate had the means to do so, you can do it one further service, please, and tell me as much as you know – or should I say as much as you remember."

Phineas looked at her with parched eyes.

"Sarah," he croaked, "do you think I could have a cup of something first, please?"

Chapter Seventeen

The boyfriend, Adrian, had made the booking from their hotel in Shrewsbury. They both lived in London and were on a touring holiday.

He had phoned again then, in the morning, to confirm the booking and to detail, one chap to another, the route he intended taking to Batch Magna, a distance of some thirty odd miles. Reeling off the initials and numbers of the roads while Phineas said, "huh-huh", and "right", and "yep, yep", in a clipped sort of fashion, and thought about what to get for lunch.

Daniel, his undergraduate son, had taken Ffion Owen for a spin in the Frogeye but had said he'd be back, which, Phineas decided, probably meant three for lunch. They'd have it out on deck, on a day like this, with a bottle or two of something white and chilled to go with it.

His son was here on his usual summer visit from his home in London, where he lived with his mother and stepfather. Phineas had been married three times, leaving, among other things in their wake, four children. Daniel was the only child from his first marriage, and because his mother was the only one of his wives he still had any sort of relationship with, Daniel was the only one of those children he now saw.

But he had lately come to suspect that his son's visits were now largely made out of habit. He had come to feel something like embarrassment growing between them, their worlds, who Phineas was and his life here, and the young man Daniel, overnight it seemed, had become, turning them into polite strangers to each other.

Adrian then had to ask if he was still there. Phineas had been thinking about the choice of wine.

Adrian said it again, he said that, looking at the map, he didn't see that he could shave any more time off the journey, and what did he, Phineas, who presumably knew the area, think? Phineas agreed completely. He said no, he couldn't see any slack there either, couldn't see how Adrian could tighten up the time any further. It was, he added for good measure, exactly the route he would have taken.

After all, Adrian sounded as if he knew what he was talking about. He, Phineas, hadn't the foggiest. He was never in that much of a hurry to get anywhere.

And that, as he periodically had reason to observe, to himself and to others, getting quite heated about it at times, was *precisely* what was wrong with the river.

As Ratty knew. Whether boating up and down it, or simply sitting on it, whether you get away or whether you don't, whether you arrive at your destination or somewhere else entirely, or whether you never get anywhere at all. There never was any particular hurry to go anywhere or do anything.

He decided on cold meats, cheese, pickled gherkins, French rolls and salad, that sort of thing, and a couple of bottles of Riesling to go with it.

Chapter Eighteen

The village pub, the Steamer Inn, a paddler puffing busily away on its sign, was built in 1662, and called the Black Boy, in honour of their restored monarch, Charles II, until Sir Cosmo Strange brought the paddle steamers home.

There was memorabilia from those days on a wall in the saloon bar, the larger of the pub's two bars. Copies of sailing bills and freight charges, advertisements, tickets, and photographs of the paddle steamers, smoke idling, the crews in emblazoned sweaters and ribboned caps, and Sir Cosmo in a silk topper, fob watch in hand, the passengers, in their best bonnets and Sunday bowlers, waiting on the landing stage of what was now part of the *Batch Castle's* moorings, and one of the Silver Band from Church Myddle playing on the inaugural trip, and the first herd of sheep being loaded, dogs low at their heels.

Phineas, dressed for punting in a straw boater, with, by now, a few wilting flowers in the ribbon, white flannels and a waistcoat colourful enough to win admiration from Humphrey, was up at the bar, playing a boisterous game of spoof with Ken Hollywell, Owain and John Beecher. While Sikes with Bryn, Owain's dog, was sprawled in front of the big empty summer fireplace, as if drowsy with a memory of its winter heat.

Phineas had told Adrian how to get to the *Belle* once they arrived in Batch Magna. What he hadn't told him was how to get to Batch Magna once they arrived in Batch Valley. Instead of ten o'clock, as arranged, it was nearly eleven when he and his girlfriend Suzanne walked into the bar, neither looking particularly happy to be doing so.

And then Suzanne saw Phineas and smiled. And for Phineas the sun came out.

"We tried the other bar first," she said. "They said you'd be in here. Wearing a boater."

Phineas removed it.

"And you, I take it, are *Su-zanne*," he breathed, lingering over the name, and resting the hat on his heart. Suzanne was wearing white linen short shorts and she was long-legged, and her sleeveless, lime-green cross-over top was tied a few inches above her slender, tanned waist, the silk material snug hammocks for her breasts. And she shone, her short dark hair and eyes liquid with light, her skin golden.

"You got my note, then …?" he said, gazing at her.

"Yes," Adrian cut in. "*Eventually.*"

"Ah, good," Phineas said, reluctantly including him in it, and muttered something about unforeseen circumstances.

"And this is Adrian," Suzanne said, her smile losing some of its wattage. "And you're Phineas," she added, the sun coming out again.

"Yes …" he said, smiling foolishly back at her. "Yes …"

And then remembering his manners introduced the three others.

Adrian nodded his way brusquely through the introductions. Adrian had also been in the sun, but on him it was merely a suntan.

Phineas lifted his head as if looking down a gun sight, and trained his novelist's eye on him.

Adrian had gone for the artisan's look of corduroys and a collarless denim shirt, and his face had a sort of complacent cleverness about it, a finished sort of look, as if life, and probably his mother before that, had convinced him that no further improvement was necessary. Phineas knew the type. He'd used a couple of them in his crime novels. They always knew best and always took the *Guardian*. And they *never* got out alive.

He turned his attention back to Suzanne. "You have, if I may say so, Suzanne, a perfectly lovely smile. It should, in my humble opinion, be framed, and hung in the National Whatnot."

"Well, thank you, Phineas," she said on a laugh. "I just hope we're not too late for the trip."

"Never!" he assured her, and putting his punter's hat on again, gave the crown a decisive tap, dislodging a couple of blooms from the ribbon. He brushed them off a shoulder, mere flowers in Suzanne's presence.

Adrian snorted.

"It's hardly our fault if we were. I was *right* on schedule until I got to the turn-off for this place. Then we got *completely* lost. The lanes round here …! Talk about Hampton Court Maze. I would," he said directly to Phineas, "have appreciated being given at least *some* idea of how to get here."

Phineas took it on the chin.

"You're quite right, old man, quite right. It was remiss of me, and you are owed an official apology. Which I now issue. Without quibble."

"We had to stop at a farmhouse for directions – and then had to write them down," Suzanne said, looking amused by it.

"It can be difficult," John Beecher said politely, "finding your way round here."

Adrian spread his hands in disbelief. "And not a signpost to be seen. Not one," he said, shaking his head over it.

"Well, no need for 'em, see," Ken explained. "Everybody here knows the way." He had put on his Sunday suit for the occasion of his daughter's birth, a couple of fountain pens on display in his top pocket, and his best flat cap.

Adrian looked at him. "And what about people who *don't* know the way?" he pointed out, and Ken frowned, as if he hadn't thought of that. "Like us, for example. I mean," Adrian went on with a small laugh, "surely you get visitors here sometimes, don't you? Holidaymakers or whatever?"

"Anyway, we're here now," Suzanne said, doing the smiling for both of them.

"We get lots of visitors," Owain said, sensing a criticism of his village.

"Well, if we do I never see them," Patrick the landlord put in. He was crouched on a stool, drawing off four pints of Sheepsnout from the wooden barrel behind the bar, the name of the cider stamped on it like a warning.

"The gentleman milking the nectar there is Patrick," Phineas said, "who runs this establishment with his wife, Dilly, the lady you no doubt saw in the other bar."

"The gossip shop," John Beecher added.

Phineas introduced the couple and Patrick smiled over his shoulder at them, a smile not without sympathy. He had heard all about the punting business, and was a man with long experience of Phineas.

Adrian, who had nodded his way through that introduction as well, said in a 'and another thing' sort of voice, "And there are no street lights in the village!"

"Well – " Ken started.

"I know, don't tell me," Adrian got in. "There's no need for them. Everybody knows where everybody else lives."

"Well, they do," Ken said.

"And anyway," Owain said, "it so happens that the parish council have been having discussions about that."

"The parish council," John Beecher said, "have been having discussions about it for as long as I can remember. It comes up regular as clockwork, every year."

"Yes, I remember getting quite excited at the prospect when I first heard of it," Patrick added, putting the first of the pints on the bar, "a few weeks after we took over here. And that was over twenty years ago now."

"Well, it's a big decision, Pat. A lot of money involved," Owain said, unwilling to accept the criticism in front of strangers.

"Never mind," Suzanne said, "there's a lovely moon out."

"All part of the service," Phineas told her, and wondered what on earth the man wanted with lights of any sort with a dazzler like Suzanne on his arm.

Adrian looked at the pints lined up on the bar, and then, pointedly, at his watch.

"Look," Phineas said, "I lost the last round of spoof, the game we were playing, so I'm obliged to buy the drinks. Now, won't you join us? Just a quick one for the river, then we'll punt away like mad, I promise."

"You'll be doing that right enough – if you get it wrong tonight, the way it's running," Owain said. And because the Hall's punt had been considered too small for the venture, it was Owain's fishing punt that would be out on it.

Adrian was frowning. "Have we got time for this?"

"Oh, *come* on, Adrian," Suzanne said. "We're on holiday. One drink won't hurt. And the boat can hardly go without us, can it?"

And Suzanne smiled at Adrian, offering a truce, and Adrian relented and smiled at Suzanne. And Phineas, Captain of a Romantic Evening on a Punt for Two, smiled on them both. This was their night, and he determined there and then that he was jolly well going to make sure it was a memorable one.

"Good man," he said, slapping Adrian's back. "And it is something of a special occasion. Ken here is a new father. His wife, Wendy, has very cleverly produced a baby girl. Their first child."

"Oh! Congratulations," Suzanne said.

"Ah," Ken said complacently. "Her calved down this afternoon." He grinned, foolish with pride and half a gallon of Sheepsnout. "Fat as butter, her is, the little one. Seven pounds two ounce, her weighs."

"And is everything all right?"

"Oh, ah. Her's fine. Both of 'em is."

While Ken told Suzanne, a fresh audience, how he'd held his baby daughter for the first time, and how, not a man to buy a pig in a poke, he had sneaked a look to check that all her toes, as well as her fingers, were there, Adrian unbuttoned a back pocket of his trousers, and unzipping what to Phineas looked suspiciously like a purse, wordlessly handed him the punting fee.

"Right, kids, what will you have?" Phineas said expansively, immediately richer by ten pounds. "Something you've always wanted, m'dear, and never been able to afford," he said, leering at Suzanne and brushing a finger under imaginary moustaches.

Suzanne laughed. "Is that cider?" she asked, nodding at the pints on the bar, the light in them gleaming a milky gold.

"Indeed it is," Phineas agreed. "That's Sheepshake– or Sheepsnout, as some people insist."

John Beecher laughed. "Especially if sober."

"It's local tack, Miss, from our own orchards," Patrick told her. "It's fairly strong, but there's not an impurity in it. The apples are pulped and then left to get on with it, to ferment in their own juices."

"It's from Dotty Snape's smallholding," John said, as if having trouble with his teeth. He reached for his fresh pint, frowning, trying to remember how many that would make.

"Well, when in Rome do as the Romans do," Suzanne said. She asked for a pint, and Adrian a half, because he had to drive back.

"Quite right, old man. Quite right," Phineas approved.

He lifted his glass when Patrick had finished the round. "We've toasted the newly arrived Miss Hollywell till she's up to her little pink ears in the stuff. So here's to the making of memories. And all who sail in her."

Chapter Nineteen

The Steamer Inn was a pub that made up its own closing times, and it was long past midnight when they made their way along Upper Ham, Bill Sikes trailing along behind, sniffing and lifting a leg here and there.

Adrian stopped at their car, parked halfway up on the verge in front of the *Belle*. While Phineas waited, smiling vaguely, he took a sweater from the back seat and handed Suzanne a cardigan.

"I said you'd need this."

Suzanne draped it over her shoulders and said that it had got a bit chilly.

"Well, we're on the river, darling." Adrian said. "And it's *late*," he added, his head appearing through the neck of the sweater, and looking pointedly at Phineas.

It was wasted on Phineas. He was on holiday from such pettiness, in a world lit by Sheepsnout, on a punt of his own, drifting carelessly downriver.

Their car was parked behind his Sprite, which meant that Daniel, who'd borrowed it again for the evening, was back, and probably in bed. He led the way through the mooring's makeshift gate, a farm pallet top secured, when in the closed position, with orange baler twine.

The ground in front of the *Belle* had once been a small cider orchard, some of its mossy, ancient trees, almost denuded of leaves, stood still, bent low as if by winds, their shadows reaching now across the grass as an owl called from Mawr Wood, crooked storybook shadows under a moon.

"An owl," Phineas said dreamily, and unnecessarily, and fell over his dustbin.

He cursed and picked himself up. "If I had known I was going to be this late," he said indignantly, rubbing a knee, "I'd have taken a blasted torch with me."

Adrian switched one on.

"I picked it up from the car."

"And you were waiting, I suppose, for one of us to fall in the river first, before producing it."

Adrian gave a short laugh, a man about to come out on top.

"Well, I naturally assumed that you'd know your way around your own backyard. I mean, we know you haven't had too much to drink. You were quite adamant about that when I suggested it might be the case, and that you might like to sleep if off and we'd do it tomorrow night instead."

"Adrian!" Suzanne admonished.

Phineas drew himself up. "I resented the implication then, and I resent it now," he said stiffly.

"More a statement, rather than an implication, I would have thought. Still, you're the writer, you tell us, so you'd know."

If there was an answer to that Phineas was having trouble thinking of it.

"Are we just going to stand here?" Suzanne wanted to know.

"It does not do to entertain thoughts of dumping a customer in the river," Phineas said then, addressing the air, and as if quoting from a manual.

"Oh, good," Suzanne said. "Then if you two children have quite finished, perhaps we can get on."

Adrian snorted a laugh, making it quite clear who he thought would end up in the river, and the two men stood glaring at each other.

Suzanne found a distraction. "Oh, look!" she said brightly.

And Phineas did, and instantly forgot about Adrian.

"How can *anyone*," he appealed to her, "be expected to look *anywhere*, but at you when you smile like that?"

"Phineas – *honestly!*" she protested, and prettily trilled a laugh.

"Look at *what?*" Adrian barked at her.

She sighed. "The lights, Adrian. On the boat there. I think they're pretty," she explained, heavily, as if that was the last thing she expected him to understand.

The two lamps hanging from the deck stanchions either side of the gangway shone in the dark, the colour of jewels.

Good old Dan, Phineas thought, leaving them on to guide the old man his weary way home, and he felt a pang again at what he saw as their growing apartness.

At the difference he had become aware of lately, between the young boy who had played there in past summers, as carefree and as unquestioning as a young animal, and the rather serious, and, he suspected, when it came to his father, censorious young man he had become. The past, he'd thought, coming home to roost.

This was, he imagined, one of the last, or maybe even the last, visits his son would make there.

"They're underway lamps, Suzanne," he told her. "Green for starboard, red for port, and keep a weather eye and the wardroom open."

"You're not trying to tell us that these old tubs still work," Adrian said.

"Well, they've still got their paddle wheels," Suzanne said, wandering down towards the boat, sitting becalmed in still, deep shadows, its upperworks drenched in moonlight.

Phineas had told her all about the houseboats, and had given her a tour of the Cluny Steamboat Company's history on the wall of the pub, while Adrian discussed the fastest route to Aberystwyth with the other men at the bar.

"I wouldn't be at all surprised, on a night like this," Phineas said, "if she *did* still work. In fact, I wouldn't be at all surprised if I didn't end up taking you back in her, chugging up to Shrewsbury in the moonlight. *We were chugging along on Moonlight Bay*," he warbled, and then put a finger to his lips. "*Shhh*! My son's asleep."

"Must have been great, taking a trip on her," Suzanne said, gazing up at the deck.

"Come aboard and have a look," Phineas invited.

"What about your son?" she said.

"Be all right. Long as we're quiet. He'll be tucked up sound asleep in his little camp bed," he said, smiling foolishly at a memory from another time, and another place, quietly closing the door after a bedtime reading of his son's favourite book, *The Wind in the Willows*.

Adrian sighed heavily. "Shouldn't we be getting on?"

"Plenty of time, Andy. *Plenty* of time," Phineas said airily, leading the way up the gangway.

"Adrian," Adrian reminded him over Suzanne's shoulder.

"*Shhh*!" Phineas hissed back, and then up on deck saw there was a single light burning in the sitting room. "He's still awake," he whispered. "That's his reading lamp. He works late sometimes, studying. In there," he added, pointing a finger at the sitting room as if to make it perfectly clear what sitting room he was referring to.

"Perhaps we ought to leave it, Phineas," Suzanne said.

"No, no, no. Danny won't mind. Give him a break from his study books. I'll show you the galley first," he said, waving them on.

Bill Sikes, who had gone aboard ahead of them, and was now slumped on deck, waiting to be let in, followed the small procession towards the stern.

"The galley," Phineas said, opening the door to it, and tutting before closing it on the washing-up piled in the sink and on the side.

"And directly behind this is the shower room," he said, and turned to the sitting room directly opposite.

"It used to be a deck saloon, for inclement weather. It is still, in a way. My refuge and haven."

He put a finger to his lips. "Shhh. We'll just drop in and say hello," he whispered. "He's studying applied mathematics," he added, not without pride. "Whatever that is."

He opened the door quietly and Bill Sikes pushed past them and headed straight for the sofa where he normally slept, and where Daniel and Ffion Owen were now lying, locked in a desperate, fumbling embrace, and tried to clamber up on them. When it came to displays of human affection, Sikes was a dog who liked to join in.

"I thought you'd gone to bed, Dad!" Daniel said when he'd found his voice, pushing the dog off and staring aghast at the door, as if wondering how many more people were going to come through it.

"Clearly," Phineas said shortly.

"I thought he was in there with you," Daniel said, pushing Sikes off again.

"I said I thought I heard somebody," Ffion muttered, pulling her shirt over a red bra – a dangerous colour on a woman, it was Phineas's experience. And Daniel, he noticed, had borrowed his blue striped business shirt, the one that went with his overdraft suit.

"That chap there, in the shirt, is my son, Daniel, and the young lady is Ffion Owen, daughter of Owain, whom you met in the pub," he said making the introductions, while the couple on the sofa, their backs turned to the visitors, fiddled furiously with buttons.

He then showed Suzanne and Adrian the bedroom at the end of the sitting room, shaking his head at the clothes strewn about as if someone else were to blame, before closing the door on it.

He tutted and shook his head again then, leading them back past the chastened-looking pair on the sofa, Bill Sikes sitting upright between them like a chaperon.

"I don't know," he said, out on deck. "Teenagers today."

Chapter Twenty

Phineas led the way down to what he called the punting station, the bank astern of the paddler, where Owain's fourteen-foot Wyre fishing punt was tied up with the *Belle's* dinghy.

He pulled the punt in, side on to the bank, and held it steady while they climbed gingerly aboard, the boat moving under them.

"Mind the stick, m'dears," he said, referring to the punting pole resting lengthways on it. "Don't want that disappearing overboard."

The light from Adrian's torch moved over the craft and found the seat at the bow end, padded with purple cushions with yellow piping and tassels from the Owens' rowing skiff.

"Park your bums," Phineas said breezily, climbing in after them.

"That's it, make yourselves at home."

He lit the storm lantern he'd placed mid-boat, and turned the wick up, the white light flaring in the glass.

He beamed at them over it. "What *fun* this is!"

"They're supposed to be coloured," Adrian pointed out.

Phineas muttered something about local rags and misprints, and lit the second lamp, near the stern. And watched as the glass started to blacken.

"Perhaps it needs a new wick," Suzanne suggested.

"Probably just needs trimming," Adrian said with off-hand authority, sitting back against the cushions with an arm around her.

Phineas coughed and waved away smoke seeping from under the top of the glass.

"No, Suzanne's quite right – women often, if not always, are. We'll turn it off. Don't want to risk a fire. The hull's got more tar on it than the M1. Well, we may have lost a lamp but we're still afloat, that is the main thing on the river – as indeed it is in life more generally. Comfortable?"

"Emm ..." Suzanne murmured.

The night smelt of summer and the river. A tawny owl called again from Mawr Wood on the opposite bank, its drawn-out cry drifting across the bat-haunted air. And high above the willows a yellow moon sat, as fat as butter, in the shining dark with its face in the water, the river running with its light midstream as if it were dissolving there. Under the trees the shadows were black, deeper pools.

"What is that?" Suzanne asked, ear cocked.

"What, the owl?" Phineas said. "It's an *owl*, Suzanne."

"No, no, not that. Listen ..."

"I can't hear anything."

He peered down at the floor of the punt.

"It's not a sort of glug-glug sound, is it? Oh, good," he said, when told it wasn't.

"Well, it could be almost anything. There's a whole night shift beavering away on the banks. It could be woodpigeons, seeing that it's a full moon. They coo at it, thinking it's a new day. Then the silly things have to do it all again in the morning. Or bats. Up there, look. Out after a bite of supper. I'm too old now to hear them. It is a well-known fact," he pontificated, "that only the very young can pick up the squealing of a Baubenton's water bat. It's a glass slipper which fits no one much over the age of twenty," he said, opening the cardboard box holding the wine and glasses.

Suzanne, nearer thirty, smiled in an interested sort of way and said nothing.

"Well, I can hear them, and I'm thirty-two," Adrian said, but Phineas wasn't stopping for details.

"It's among the other things only the very young can tune into. The sort of thing that some of us never stop hearing – or at any rate never stop listening for."

"Is that supposed to mean anything?" Adrian asked with a derisive laugh.

"What, on a night like this? Certainly not!" Phineas said, popping a cork on one of the two dry whites. He could not bear to stint, and had added a second bottle out of his own pocket to go with the one included in the fee.

"Actually, Phineas," Suzanne said, "it's more like a whistling sound than squealing ... There –there it is again."

"Otters," Phineas said immediately. "Otters, Suzanne. There's a holt, a burrow, downstream a bit, on what's called Snails Eye Island, the home of a bitch otter and her cubs. She spends hours whistling at them, telling them to do this, and not to do that, and to come in, your tea's ready, and wash your paws first, all that sort of thing. There's no dog otter. The female of the species treats the male *appallingly*," he went on, making his way forward with the bottle and two glasses. "She whistles the poor fellow up, lets him have his way with her, and then shows him the door. Wham, bam, thank you, Dan, as it were. A little fuel for the trip," he said, pouring the wine. "I'll leave the bottle."

"What about you?" Suzanne said.

Phineas held up a stern hand.

"No. It's very considerate of you, my dear girl, but no. This, Suzanne, is where I hand the night over to you. It is now yours. Yours and Andy's alone."

"Adrian's," Adrian said, more to himself.

"The memories you will make together on this river, my gift to you both."

"*Ahhh!*" Suzanne said. "That's nice. Isn't that nice, Adrian?"

Adrian opened his mouth to give his view on it, but Phineas wasn't stopping.

"I must now," he said, sweeping off his boater, "leave the stage. I have, as it were, brought the curtain up, and must now take my place behind the scenes. A mere pusher and puller of things, unseen and unheard."

"Fat chance of that," Adrian said. "Look, do you think we could actually get started? At this rate –"

"Shhh!" Suzanne said.

"Easy to see he's got no competition in the area," Adrian muttered.

"The oarsman to those memories you will make. A steerer of dreams under the stars. A gondolier in the night."

Phineas took a bow to Suzanne's applause, and clapping his boater back on, exited to his place in the stern.

He uncoupled the mooring chain from the ring on the punting deck, and chucked it up on the bank, ready for their return. And then tossed a pair of short oars after it.

"Shan't need *those*."

"What are they?" Adrian asked suspiciously.

"Paddles," Phineas said. "For steering. How's the wine?"

"Super!" Suzanne said.

"That was my verdict. I sampled a bottle earlier – on your behalf, of course. Not the most expensive wine in the shop, I grant you, but surprisingly good, I thought."

"You'll be seeing pink elephants, the way you drink."

Suzanne pulled away from him. "Adrian! You're so *rude*!"

"I find life thirsty work, old man," Phineas said equably. "And besides, what have you got against pink elephants?"

"Yes, they're nice cuddly things," Suzanne said. "Not like some people I could name. Cheers, Phineas!" she cried gaily.

"Happy days, old thing," Phineas said, poking at the bank with the punting pole.

Chapter Twenty-One

"Well, that's all right then," Adrian said to her, as the boat started to bob away from the bank. "Because you'll probably be seeing them yourself in the morning, the way you've been throwing it back."

Suzanne glared at him, and finishing her drink in one, thrust the glass at him. Adrian sighed heavily. He poured, and then filled and drained his own.

"Now look who's talking about throwing it back."

"When in Rome do as the Romans do," he said, echoing Suzanne earlier.

"You can be so childish! Well, quite frankly, Adrian, if you're going to keep on like this, I don't see any point in our being here. In fact, I don't see any point in continuing the holiday at all. We might as well go straight back to London."

"Now, now, you chaps!" Phineas said, jollying them along while sinking the pole into the water before it went any further. If it came to a refund, he wasn't sure if there was anything left *to* refund.

Standing on the punting deck, he was turning the boat from the stern to face towards the opposite bank. He had to cross the river to go up it, avoiding a low, tilting over-hang of alders some yards up on their side, and beyond that the wreckage of the *PS Sabrina*. He had also to navigate the strong midstream current, a current which was even stronger now, after the rain – as Owain had made a point of reminding him at least twice that evening. Owain seemed to have a thing about that current, chuntering on about it when giving him lessons on the right way to cross it as if he, Phineas, had never been on the river before, as if he'd never used that same current to give him a push when rowing back downriver in his dinghy. Just because he'd be doing it with a punting pole instead of oars.

Adrian was murmuring now in the shadows, words for Suzanne's ears only. Phineas was encouraged. Unless he was threatening her with murder, and understandably didn't want a witness to it, he was making amends. And judging by her silence, she was perhaps willing to have amends made. The fee, it seemed, or whatever was left of it, was safe.

Standing as close to the water as he could without falling in it, as Owain had taught him, he dropped the pole again, skimming the edge of the deck with it, and letting it fall under its own weight, sixteen foot of polished spruce, between lightly ringed fingers.

The Cluny wasn't a particularly deep river, which had suited the shallow-draught vessels of the Cluny Steamboat Company, and the pole touched bottom halfway down its length.

He lifted it clear of the water, the varnished wood dripping light.

He dropped it again and lifted, dropped and lifted, pushing out steadily towards midstream.

And doing so, if he did say so himself, with remarkable smoothness.

Apart from the odd time at school, messing about on the Thames at Windsor, and the few lessons he'd had beforehand from Owain, he had never really punted before. But there was no getting away from it, he was a natural. This, he told himself, was punting as it was spoke.

He felt as much connected to the river as he was to the punt, as much below the surface as he was above it, an inhabitant of some new dimension he'd found somewhere between the two.

He glanced over at the couple in the bow. The shadows there had merged into one. That was more like it! That was what they were *supposed* to be doing. A boy and girl in a punt in the moonlight. That was what it was supposed to add up to.

"*You can't beat the memories you gave me. They're sweet those memories you gave me...*" he crooned, a gondolier in the night.

"Any more wine, Phineas?" Suzanne called then.

"Coming up," he said cheerily.

He shipped the pole, hoisting it in the air with drill-like precision, before lowering it smartly on the punt, as if following an old formality.

Adrian, watching this, said, "I'd better get it."

"No, no, no, you stay there, Andy. I'll do it, wearing my wardroom steward's hat."

Tra-la-la-ing away, Phineas set about pulling the cork on the second bottle of white, the punt idly drifting.

Lightly tripping his way forward, as nimble as a gondolier, he missed a step and his foot came down hard on the side of the boat.

"Oops! Point to starboard there, as my friend the Commander would say."

Adrian grabbed for the gunnel that side, the punt rocking, and Phineas laughed briefly and indulgently at the sight of a landlubber with the wind up.

"Where are we going?" Suzanne asked lazily from the shadows, the punt moving through the water again, spreading ripples of moonlight in its wake.

"Where would you like to go?" Phineas said. "Name it, and we'll go there. Trailing stars."

And he wouldn't be at all surprised at that. On such a night as this he felt that anything was possible, anything might happen.

They scarcely intruded on its bright stillness, moving through it with so little sound and effort that he might almost have been dreaming it, the river murmuring and gurgling softly as it did many times in his sleep. A couple of feeding mallards paddled, hissing, out of their path, and a swan, its wings starched with light, glided out to see what the vulgar fuss was about, before making its stately way back to the shadows under the fronds of a weeping willow.

And the shining pole was dropped and lifted, dropped and lifted again, breaking the water as quiet as a fish rising.

He hardly felt he was doing any work at all —as if he *had* to do any work. He felt that the punt could carry on perfectly well without him, could make its own way to wherever it was going, to wherever it was taking them.

Languor and enchantment, that was the essence, the very *essence*, of punting, he decided dreamily, and felt the sudden bump and pull of the midstream current as the boat met it bow on.

Chapter Twenty-Two

He'd forgotten about the midstream current. He was supposed to be crossing it at a 45 degrees angle, he remembered, now it was too late. He was supposed to be gliding across it, letting whatever the ruddy hell Owain had said do the work for him. What he *wasn't* supposed to be doing was the other thing Owain had said – the other thing he remembered him saying – the thing he was now doing, because he couldn't think what else *to* do. Dancing about on the deck, pushing the pole in first one side and then the other, the punt wallowing and swinging this way and that.

The night looked far more ordinary now and, with the boat slowly but steadily being pulled downstream, increasingly predictable.

"I'll get seasick in a minute," Adrian said.

"Do you know anything about punting, old man?" Phineas muttered tightly.

"No," Adrian had to admit, "as a matter of fact, I don't."

"No, I thought not. Well, this is a punting technique for traversing a strong midstream current. Get the angle wrong and you'll find yourself drifting downriver," he puffed, quoting the other thing he remembered Owain saying.

"Aren't we doing that already?" Adrian asked a few moments later.

"Aren't we doing *what*?" Phineas snapped.

"Drifting downriver – if, that is, downriver's that way."

"Downriver *is* that way. But I can assure you, Andy, that we are not drifting anywhere I do not want us to drift. All right? That okay with you …?"

"If you say so. And it's Adrian. Not Andy. Of course, I realise I'm the wrong sex, but you might at least try and get my name right, seeing as I'm a paying customer."

But Phineas was no longer listening.

The river there was a mixture of stone and mud. And he had found the mud, the pole going in a clear couple of feet, judging by what was left at his end of it. He had driven it down hard out of nothing but sheer frustrated temper, and now the mud had it. And it wasn't letting go.

"Are you all right, Phineas?" Suzanne asked, concerned curiosity in her voice.

He had turned his back on them and was surreptitiously trying to tug it free, his shoulders heaving as if laughing, or sobbing.

"Yes, yes, I'm fine," he said testily. "Thank you for asking!"

"We're stuck," Adrian told her. "We're stuck on something. What are we stuck on?"

"We are not stuck on anything." Phineas had tried for amused exasperation, a professional dealing with a fretful amateur, but he was almost grunting with the strain, sweat leaking from under his boater.

He was about to let the mud have it, about to act on the other piece of advice he remembered Owain giving him – if in trouble, hang on to the punt and not the pole. When it came free, suddenly.

He staggered back with it, and then lurched forward to avoid toppling into the boat, lifting it like a pole vaulter and driving it into the river again, to stop himself going overboard. He hit stone this time and pushed violently on it, past caring what happened.

The punt, thrust free of the current, bobbed gently into a stretch of slack water.

Phineas rested on his pole, puffing and blowing, taking his hat off to wipe at the sweat.

"That's always the trickiest bit – that cross current," he told them, shaking his head over it. "Even without all the rain we've had recently, it's been the undoing of a few good watermen in the past, I can tell you. It's famous for it. All calm on the surface, but underneath – phew, watch out!" Just like some women he could name, he thought.

"Well done, Phineas!" Suzanne said.

"I thought we were about to capsize," Adrian said, his tone suggesting that in his opinion they were lucky not to.

Phineas sighed.

"My dear fellow," he began with heavy patience. "My dear good fellow, you can hole a punt. You can set fire to a punt. You can take an axe to a punt. You can blow a punt out of the water. But what you cannot – absolutely can*not* do, is to capsize one. It simply can't be done. Its proportions should tell you that. It's *impossible* to overturn, not in the normal way of things. That's the reason, of course," he added on a more matey note, with the danger now past, "why it's the ideal craft for a bit of you-know-what."

"No, I don't know what," Adrian said perversely.

Suzanne gave him a dig with her elbow. "You could have fooled me!"

"Suzanne!"

"Don't you Suzanne me, you little devil. Cheers, Phineas!" she cried.

"Cheers, m'dears," Phineas said, poling on upstream, and wondering if there was anything else he should be remembering to do, or not to do.

There was a tinkle of bottle and glasses, and silence from the bow end.

And then Suzanne said, "In fact, Adrian, I sometimes feel that's all I'm good for."

"Now, you know that's not true."

"Do I? Do I, Adrian?"

"It's just the drink talking. You know perfectly well – " Adrian glanced over at the stern and lowered his voice.

But Phineas wasn't interested in what he had to say – he'd heard it all before, whatever it was. He'd said it himself enough times. Besides, it was nothing to do with him, what did he know? He was only the driver.

And anyway, he had a bit of company himself now, a sheep up on one of the fields tracking him between the trees, before giving up on the idea that his appearance meant food. It was one of Vernon Watkins's fields, the grass stiffened like frost with moonlight, the sheep out on it as still as stones.

Until Phineas stirred them up.

Vernon, he knew, had had a late lambing, and, as usual, a good crop of them. It was a well-known fact that Vernon had the randiest ram in the valley. Pan, his name was, and once he had started he didn't stop until he'd run out of ewes. Lambing took no time at all when Pan was on the job.

"*I'm a well-endowed ram and I got where I am by performing my act right on cue. When it's time for a tup, I just line 'em all up, and shout volunteers? Ewe, ewe and ewe,*" he sang, giving it a Gilbert & Sullivan air, and finishing to a chorus of bleating from a growing audience of ewes and lambs.

Encouraged, he had just started on *Old Macdonald had a Farm*, a party of one his end of the punt, when Adrian, after a few tries, got through to him.

"That's better! *Thank* you –we're trying to talk here ..."

"I don't think there's any more to talk about," Suzanne said. "I thought this trip might help clear the air. It hasn't. I still don't know where I stand."

That was something else Phineas had heard before, only last week, from his girlfriend, Sally.

He felt a stab of contrition at the thought of her, and rested on his pole to consider it, while the couple bickered on in the bow.

His trouble, he told himself, was that he didn't know when he was well off. Most men would have stopped there, once a smasher like Sally came into their lives. Sorry, they'd have said, the position's now taken. But not him. Oh no! He had a golden bird, as it were, like Sally in the hand, and had to go beating the bushes for more. He didn't deserve her.

She'd been right in her suspicions about the woman with the fishing shop in Kingham. Her childish– as he'd described them then–references to flies and tackle all too near the mark. He admitted that now, owned up to it. And resolved there and then that from now on things would be very different. He felt better already.

"Andy – Andy," he said, passing it on, "we, the male of the species, can be absolute rotters!"

"Speak for yourself," Adrian said, breaking off his muttered discussion with Suzanne.

"It behoves us to play up and play the game," Phineas announced, sharing with him the view from his new-found moral heights. "And to play that game, Andy, with a straight bat on a level wicket. We should remember," he further advised him, quoting at least one of his ex-wives, "that in every relationship there are two people."

"That's very true," Suzanne agreed.

"In tandem together. Both going the same way."

"Well, if you're on a tandem," Adrian couldn't resist pointing out, "you *have* to go the same way."

Phineas ignored it. "Love– love, Andy, is a bicycle made for two."

"*Daisy, Daisy, give me your answer do,*" Adrian sang, not at all cheerfully.

"*Shhh*!" Suzanne hissed.

"Well – what rot! And he knows it," he said, jabbing a finger at Phineas. "It's all flannel."

But Phineas was elsewhere, firing on Sheepsnout and a new perspective.

"The male should bring to a relationship maturity, responsibility and commitment," he went on, addressing the air and counting out the requirements with a finger.

"He should be prepared to shoulder his share of the work involved, as well as the fun – and the *you*-know-what," he added, glancing sharply at Adrian, his tone suggesting that not only did he find the expression objectionable, but that it was Adrian who had first used it.

"Peddling up the hills of that relationship together, as well as freewheeling down them in the good times with the wind in one's hair."

"Sounds like a shampoo ad," Adrian said.

"Oh, be quiet, Adrian!" Suzanne said, flapping a hand at him.

"Phineas," she said solemnly, "I think that's very wise. And beautifully put."

"Pl – *ease*!" Adrian said.

"I don't expect you to understand, Adrian."

"It's from the heart, Suzanne," Phineas said. "A lesson learned at last." And he couldn't *wait* to tell Sally.

"It's something you could do with thinking about," she told Adrian.

"*What*! For god's sake – what a load of …!"

"Is it? Is it, Adrian?" she asked, and laughed bitterly.

"Well – well, in that case, maybe you'd prefer him sitting with you, instead of me."

"Maybe I would – but not for the reasons you think. It might surprise you to know, Adrian, that some men are capable of feelings above their belts."

Adrian shot to his feet. "Right! That's it! Come on, then, Phineas," he said, on his way to the stern, rocking the punt in his haste to get there, "you can take my place. You can talk rubbish to her while I do the punting."

"Now, don't be silly," Phineas said, "there's a good chap."

"Nothing silly about it. You heard her. So come on, hand over the pole, or whatever it's called."

"Bit of a tiff, that's all. She didn't mean it."

"Oh, yes she did!" Suzanne said. "I don't want him sitting with me. Now or at any other time. As far as I'm concerned that's it. It's finished."

"Just what I was thinking," Adrian said to her. "Off you go," he added to Phineas.

"Now –"

"Come on, Phineas, leave him to it," Suzanne said. "Come and keep me company."

Phineas held on to the pole, his eyes darting between the two.

"It's not my punt," he said then, as if in appeal. "Even if I wanted to, I've no authority to."

"Oh, well," Suzanne said, "if you don't *want* to."

"It's not that. I didn't mean that, it's just – "

"You're not going anywhere, are you?" Adrian pointed out. "You'll still be here, technically in charge of the vessel, won't you?"

"You've been drinking," Phineas said, coming up with another objection.

"*I've* been drinking?" Adrian snorted a laugh.

"You don't know how to punt," Phineas said then.

"Well, I couldn't make a worse job of it than you. I doubt we've gone more than twenty yards since we started. Just tell me the basics, that's all you need do. I'm a quick study."

Phineas stared at him.

"Come on, Phineas," Suzanne called softly, her eyes beckoning from beyond the single light, where she waited in a bed of shadows.

Phineas thrust the pole at him.

"Well, what do I have to do?" Adrian asked, Phineas already on his way to the bow, the punt rocking again.

"What? Oh, nothing to it, old man. Couldn't be simpler. Just push downwards and backwards with the pole, at a sort of angle, you know, to get it going again, and then lift it and drop it again, and then– well, just push away. And for extra speed, bend your knees into the down stroke. That's all there is to it. Have fun. Oh, and if you do get stuck, remember to hang on to the punt and not the stick," he added, on his way past the single lantern, moths fluttering around its light, leaving Adrian muttering to himself, going over his instructions on the punting deck.

"Now what *is* this all about? Mmm?" he said, parking himself next to Suzanne, and patting her hand.

"How am I doing then?" Adrian asked complacently a while later.

"Fine, Andy, you're doing fine," Phineas said absently. As the same sex as Adrian, he was learning what a swine he was, holding Suzanne's hand and murmuring sympathetically now and then.

"Yes, well, it's not exactly difficult, is it," Adrian said on a laugh. "I mean, it would be hard to find a more basic form of propulsion."

"No, you're doing splendidly, Andy, splendidly. Couldn't do better myself," Phineas muttered, gazing at Suzanne.

Even her teeth shone, gleaming moistly in the reflected light as she smiled at him. She smiled at him, and he smiled at her, and before he knew what was happening it had happened. They had kissed.

And if the earth didn't move, then the punt did, rolling, unnoticed, under them.

"Soon got that sorted," Adrian told himself then.

The punt and the midstream current had suddenly met again, and he wasn't sure how it had happened, but after splashing about with the pole, trying to use it as a rudder to steer with, he found himself facing what he was sure was the other way.

Up or down river, what did it matter? He'd got out of trouble midstream in half the time it had taken Phineas – and *he* was supposed to be the professional. He sank the pole in again and gave a scornful laugh in Phineas's direction.

Not that Phineas noticed. Phineas was lost, to Sally and the new perspective, drowning in Suzanne, and going down for the third time, the third, lingering kiss, their embrace increasingly heated and desperate with murmured endearments between more kisses.

Adrian was also enjoying himself. He had really started to motor now, as he thought of it, the current doing most of the work for him. He didn't understand why they hadn't set off downriver in the first place. He was using the current instead of fighting it, going with the flow. After that it was just a question of rhythm and balance.

He was beginning to suspect that, despite his boasting, Phineas hadn't a clue. He wondered, at this speed, and given that they were going the right way, how long it would take them to get to Shrewsbury.

They were fairly bowling along, Adrian bending his knees and pushing away. Past the houseboats and Snails Eye Island, and a sleeping Batch Magna, while his passengers grew more passionate in the shadows.

Running under the moon and the ruined castle on the hill, punting on down to the water meadows, past Magna and Lower Rea, Leech Meadow, Pistol and Prill Leasow, to where the fall of swollen water over Prill Weir ahead of them was like a storm wind gathering in the trees.

Chapter Twenty-Three

Adrian heard it first.

"What is that ...? What *is* that?" he said on a louder note.

"Mmm ...?" Phineas murmured from the bow.

"That sound. What is it?"

"An otter," Phineas said, smiling foolishly at Suzanne. "Whistling up a mate ..."

"No, it's not that. It's not a whistling sound," Adrian said to himself.

"It's not a whistling sound," he told Phineas.

"Phineas ...?"

Phineas sighed in the shadows.

"What?"

"It's not a whistling sound. It's not an otter."

"Then it's bats. Or owls. Or ducks. Or pigeons, or something. I don't know!"

"It's more like a ... like a train," Adrian decided. "And it seems to be getting nearer. We're not near a railway line, are we?" he asked, frowning.

"Phineas?"

Phineas's head shot up.

"*What!*"

"Are we near a railway line?"

"No, Andy," Phineas said heavily, "we are not near a railway line. We are miles from a railway line. The nearest railway line from here is at Church Myddle. All right? Anything else you'd like to know? Train times? Bus routes? Taxis? The nearest airport?" he went on with massive irony. "No? Oh, *good*."

"Well, if we're not near a railway line, then what is it?"

"What – is – what?" Phineas said tightly, a man running out of patience.

"That noise. If we're not near a railway line, then what is it?"

"What noise? I can't hear anything. And if I can't hear it, then I can't tell you what it is, can I? Now, if you don't mind – "

"Well, I can hear it."

"Bully for you."

"And it's definitely getting nearer."

"What is it, Phineas?" Suzanne murmured.

"Nothing, my sweet. Just Andy, imagining things."

Which was typical, absolutely *typical* of a city type at night in the country. With no traffic to listen to they start hearing things.

He went back to nibbling Suzanne's ear.

And then he put his head up again.

He could hear something himself now.

He thought he'd heard it before somewhere, and was trying to place it when he spotted a familiar-looking shape perched on a hill above the river, the jagged outline black against the sky.

"That looks like Batch Castle …"

"What is it, Phineas?" Suzanne said. "What's that noise?"

"It can't be Batch Castle … It *is* Batch Castle," he told himself then. "That's Batch Castle. That shouldn't be there!" he said, staring accusingly at it.

"That noise, what is it?" Suzanne was sitting up, alarmed now.

"That's Batch Castle! Where are we, Andy?" he demanded.

"I dunno," Adrian mumbled, sounding both worried and defensive. "Downriver somewhere, I think."

But Phineas already knew that, knew that that was where they *had* to be, with Batch Castle sitting up there on his right.

And he knew then what they were listening to. And it wasn't a train.

He shot to his feet, and stood swaying, feeling the speed of the punt, the current, under him. He could smell it now, as well, the foamy, churned river and waterweed smell.

And then he saw it ahead of them, shining in the moonlight, the back of the Cluny broken on its ridge boulders into broad bands of silver, the air above the fall a white mist of spray. A small Niagara in the night, carrying the river and over a week's weight of rainwater over the fish weir.

"Bloody hell!" Adrian gasped. "It's a – "

"Turn round! Go back! Stop!" Phineas shouted, meaning do something, anything, help!

Suzanne screamed.

Phineas stood frozen, unable to think.

"Down! Get down!" he yelled then, frantically pumping a hand towards the floor.

Adrian was about to get down, and Phineas was about to grab Suzanne's hand to pull her down, when the punt hit the boulders with a splintering sound and was bounced on its side as if trying to squeeze between two of them.

And then swinging round, it did what Phineas said it was impossible for a punt to do, and his world turned upside down.

He was flung off head first, and had time to hope it wouldn't hurt before gasping with shock in the bubbling white waters below.

His hands touched bottom, found the right way up, and he pushed off and broke the surface, spluttering, arms flailing, leaning into the torrent at an angle, as if into a wind, as he struggled blindly against it for a few moments.

Before being swept on and deposited with other bits and pieces of flotsam in the stretch of calm green water some yards down.

He scrambled to his feet, wiping his eyes and blinking, looking about him as if not only surprised to find himself still alive, but still alive and standing in three feet of water in the fish pond.

The punt was still on top of the weir, caught on one of the boulders, bobbing about on the current. He feared that they might be trapped under it, or maybe drowned in the white water, and was about to push back upstream again when he heard his name called.

They were a few yards behind him, and Adrian was carrying her to the bank, Suzanne sniffling and clinging helplessly to him.

Adrian also remarked on him still being alive. "You're still alive then," he said, his tone suggesting that he wasn't at all sure that Phineas had a right to be.

But at least he'd acknowledged him. Suzanne never even glanced at him -the man who had taught her what moonlight was for, or whatever it was she'd said, and who had been about to willingly risk his life for her.

He didn't say anything, merely shook his head sadly over it, the fickleness of women. Maintaining a dignified silence as, picking up his boater which had followed him down to the fish pond, he waded, dripping, after them.

Chapter Twenty-Four

Shelly insisted that Clem and Humphrey breakfast in style in the breakfast-room on the first floor, instead of the kitchen as they normally did, because it was Clem's birthday, the meal cooked and then brought up and served by her, looking as if her feet hurt.

This, they knew, was Shelly as the housemaid, Rose, from Upstairs, Downstairs, a series she never missed an episode of. Last week it had been Mrs Bridges the cook, overheard by Clem talking to the window cleaner over a cup of tea in the kitchen about her feet 'drawing something awful'.

"I'll cut the plug on that darn television one of these days," her son muttered, after his mother had brought the morning post up on the plate salver from the hall table, blowing a bit over it. Rose, having to keep going up and down those stairs with her legs.

After Clem had shown him the birthday cards the post had brought, Humphrey, with a cigar on and his novelty ashtray, a gift from Coney Island, with 'Rest Your Butt Here' written on it in front of him, sat looking suspiciously at an official-looking white envelope.

He wondered if it was from the electricity company, sending a disguised final demand. Phineas had warned him that the game they played when it came to final demands was not always one of cricket.

He opened it gingerly, his grin spreading as he read, and then he laughed.

Clem, who still had the curious and slightly guilty feeling that she was reading someone else's mail, looked up from a letter addressed to Lady Clementine Strange containing a request to open a primary school's sports day in a nearby village.

"Honey, listen to this. It's from a firm of Kingham solicitors, about some businessman from Birmingham, a Mr Marriott, who's interested in buying the Hall and lands pertaining to – blah, blah, blah. And he's prepared to pay well above market value for it. How about that?"

"Perhaps he wants to turn the Hall into an hotel and build a Disneyland type holiday village on the river, something of that sort," she teased.

Humphrey laughed. That had been him, all right, when first arriving in Batch Magna, crossing the bridge over the Cluny like an invasion, with plans to take over its future in his executive briefcase.

And now look at him.

Yeah, and now look at him. Still here, with the only change he'd made smiling across the table at him. And in this house with Clem, in this village and valley, he couldn't see, just *could* not see, how it was possible to be happier.

The letter ended up in the waste paper basket.

A while later, after Lady Clementine had turned back into Clem, in a Viyella shirt with a frayed collar and the riding breeches she never quite managed to get completely clean for her job at the hunt's yards, Sir Humphrey changed into the work clothes he'd been wearing for the last few days for painting the upstairs rooms and corridors after the rain damage under that section of the roofs that had been repaired.

Plans were afoot for Batch Hall to open its doors next year to the public.

Humphrey regarded himself in the bedroom mirror that evening, his black eye from the Battle of Cutterbach Wood now a pale yellow memory. He was giving what he called his New York suit, the Brooks Brothers executive suit, an airing, and wearing his Atlantic Sports Club member's tie and red Wall Street suspenders, or braces, as he had learned to call them, to go with it, his link to that other Humphrey, from another time and place. And he had to admit it, had to give it to himself – he still looked the part, still looked like he could cut the mustard, still looked like a wheel, a mover and shaker, some hotshot coming out of the sun on a deal, shooting from the executive hip.

Eat my dust, loser! the old Humphrey sneered at himself, the Humphrey who bragged and boasted and made things up, and who had promised Clem that he wouldn't anymore, because he had no need to; that Humphrey was back, in his red Wall Street suspenders.

"Bugger!" Clem said then, and the new Humphrey started guiltily.

"What have you lost, honey?" he asked attentively, making up for his lapse.

"My necklace – the Hawis Stone. I thought I'd wear it tonight, and I can't *think* where it could have got to," she muttered, frowning around anxiously at the floor.

"Ah!" she said then, clasping a hand to the front of the black dress she'd just put on, and then reaching into it. "I couldn't have closed it properly."

She produced the necklace, smiling with relief. "I really *do* not want to lose it."

"Here, let me do it." Humphrey took the ancient pendant with its single stone from her, fastened it, and then took a bite at her neck.

"Get off!" Clem said, laughing. "You know where that ends up."

"Yeah!" he said with relish.

"Well, we can't. We haven't time."

"I'd rather have you than a meal any day," he told her solemnly.

His wife laughed, fully appreciating the compliment.

"Well, you'll have to have the meal first tonight. And pudding later, if you behave yourself," she said, and tweaked his cheek.

They had a table booked for a birthday dinner in Kingham. Humphrey had to wait a few months yet for his birthday, and then, when it was his turn, it would be a table in the chippy, as he had learned to call it, in Church Myddle. He'd been introduced to fish and chips after a pub crawl one night with Sion and Phineas Cook – cod, chips and mushy peas, all eaten outside, on the street, a taste of paradise wrapped in yesterday's news.

They had two cars, Clem's red Mini and Henrietta, the wedding present from her parents, a wooden-framed Bentley shooting brake that had been in the family for as long as she could remember.

They took the brake, which was still a novelty to them. It was Humphrey's turn to drive it but, rather uneasily, he let Clem have the wheel on her birthday. Clem's idea of driving was to go as fast as possible as soon as possible.

There was no one these days to open the Hall's tall wrought-iron gates, gates that had once been run open for carriages and the first motor car of the valley, and which had long stayed open, rusted on their hinges, the lodge itself half-buried now in bramble and nettles, its roof timbers exposed, the bones of another age.

"Remember, honey, she's an old girl," Humphrey said with a small nervous laugh as Clem, up into second gear in no time, headed for the village and the road out of the valley.

Chapter Twenty-Five

The Hawis Stone disappeared from her neck again later, not long after they'd arrived at the restaurant. She was leaning over the table, about to lift her spoon from a full bowl of tomato soup, when it fell into it.

Clem gasped, glanced around furtively at the other diners, and then fished for it with a fork.

Her husband looked up from his own soup and watched with interest.

"My necklace," she told him, keeping her voice down. "It came off again. Fell in the soup."

"What?" he laughed.

She lifted it out and let it drip over the bowl. "That's the second time. It must be the clasp. It must be faulty."

Humphrey couldn't resist it. "Hey, waiter! There's a necklace in my wife's soup."

"*Shhh*! It's not funny. I'm just glad it didn't come off in the street." She regarded him solemnly. "You know what they say it would mean if it were lost?"

"Yeah, yeah, I know –a curse on the House of *Str-aange* ..." Humphrey said, waggling his fingers to go with the voice, and then chuckling, a traveller from the New World among the superstitions of the Old.

"You can laugh. But you never know about these things. I'll take it into a jeweller's first thing tomorrow, and get it repaired. I'm not risking it," she muttered to herself, wiping it on her napkin. It was the first time she had worn the pendant and it would be the last. It simply carried too much responsibility.

"*Damn,*" she swore then, and after glancing around again, started to rub at the soup stains splattered on the tablecloth.

Clem explained what had happened to the waiter who'd appeared at their table, turning on him, in a mixture of embarrassment and apology, a smile of such sweetness that he was galvanised into not only insisting on replacing the soup, napkin and table cloth, but also into offering to fix the clasp for her in the kitchen.

Clem rewarded him with another smile and politely declined the offer. There was only one place the Hawis Stone was going, and that was in her handbag. And it was staying there until she got it to the jeweller's tomorrow.

The pendant, with its single fire opal, was a Strange family heirloom dating back to Lady Hawis, the first baronet's wife. It had been bequeathed to Sarah by the late general, and Sarah, thinking it more appropriate for the wife of the current baronet to have it, had given it to Clem as a wedding present. Sarah had mentioned the legend attached to it then, that its loss would mean the discontinuance of the family at Batch Hall, doing so as if as an afterthought, and in an enlightened, jokey sort of way. Which hadn't stopped her, Clem had noticed, advising her, in an equally enlightened, jokey sort of way, to try not to lose it.

The Owens also knew about the legend, and they weren't in the least jokey about it.

Annie, her dark eyes wide with portent, advised her to put it under a floorboard or the bed, somewhere where it wouldn't have a *chance* to get lost. Owain called his wife a daft woman and said there were such things as banks these days, that's where the general had kept it, out of mischief's way, and he advised Clem in a hollow voice to do the same. Before she went and lost it, and they were all done for.

The next morning, Clem found a parking space round the corner from the jeweller's in Kingham and walked back to the shop with her passenger, Annie. They were going to look at the shops afterwards and then have coffee.

Plans which were about to be violently derailed.

They were nearing the jeweller's, Clem walking on the outside of the pavement, when she was pushed hard to one side, and her handbag ripped from her grip, Annie stumbling, almost falling against the plate glass window of a newsagent's.

Clem didn't hesitate. When she saw that her friend was all right, she slipped out of her court shoes, and as if following the rules of some sort of sport, conscientiously and determinedly gave chase.

She kept the thief's head in view as he raced along the pavement, pushing his way through the morning shoppers, her handbag clutched under an arm, Clem pounding after him, one hand holding up her skirt.

She was gaining on him, and smiled grimly at the prospect of catching him.

She came unstuck outside the kitchen shop, a shop she'd dawdled in, wistfully, a few times, gazing at the shining, white modern promise of large combined fridge-freezers, the latest washing machines and dryers, and the brazen enticement of coloured cookers with hoods.

They were having a delivery when she reached there, a small group of pedestrians pausing on the narrow pavement while one of those combined fridge-freezers was pushed and pulled into the shop.

It slowed her down and blocked her view ahead for a few moments. And when she did run on she could no longer see him.

Nor could she see him when she stopped at the first side road she came to.

She hesitated on the corner, people giving her a wide berth, while studiously pretending not to see her, this dishevelled looking large blonde in stocking feet, her skirt hitched up, blowing her hair from her flushed face, and glaring about her as if spoiling for a fight.

She decided to try the side street, pausing at the other roads and alleys leading off it, before giving up halfway down it.

It was no good. He could be anywhere.

She'd lost him. And her handbag.

And the Hawis Stone.

Chapter Twenty-Six

Summer sat on the hills of the valley in a green haze, and down on the Cluny, where the light of its brassy heat lay diluted on the riverbed, ducks paddled among the smoking yellow islands of water lilies, and swallows and swifts carried it on their wings as they hawked low over the water, feeding on the bright air.

And on the deck of the *Cluny Belle* Jeremy Bryant, a friend of Phineas's on a visit from London, in a yachting cap and white flannels, swatted something from his cheek and took another sip of chilled Chardonnay, the bottle nestling on ice in a dewy wine cooler.

Jeremy was also a crime writer and had a story to tell regarding his sales since the adaptation of his books for television, shaking his head over it as if modestly finding it amusing.

Phineas, who also seemed to find it amusing, said that he was delighted to hear it, really delighted for him.

"Well, nice of you to say so. Thanks, old chap."

Jeremy chuckled indulgently.

"Yes, they've gone through the roof. Quite extraordinary. The power of television, you know. And it *eats* the things! My agents are already breathing down my neck over the current work in progress."

Phineas, who hadn't missed the plural in 'agents', said he could imagine, and smiled on as if he'd forgotten it was there.

"Still, mustn't complain. Along with a few other, more boring things, it's already paid for the beast out there," Jeremy said, referring to the new BMW parked up outside the *Belle* with its tinted windows. "Next stop, tax exile, what?"

They shared a laugh at that, and then Jeremy took his sunglasses off and said, "No, but seriously, Phineas, I really do think it's time you considered getting back, you know."

Phineas blew out smoke from the Gauloise he'd just lit. "Back?"

"To civilisation. To where things are *at*, old lad."

"London, you mean?"

"Well, yes, of course, London. Where else?"

"Yes, well …" Phineas said vaguely.

"Yes, well," Jeremy echoed, and shook his head. "You have to get *with* things, Phineas."

"Oh, I don't know," Phineas said. "I think I'm fairly sort of –"

"I mean …" His friend laughed briefly, and looking around him dismissed it all with a sweep of his glasses. "I grant you it's very pretty and all that. Absolutely spot on for a weekend bolthole. Especially in this weather, what with the river on the doorstep and all that. Could be a bit nearer town, true, but one certainly sees the attraction. But for the *weekend*, Phineas. For the odd visit. You're not supposed to *live* here."

"Yes, I have to admit I do miss Oxford Street in the rush hour - especially on days like this. And sitting in a tunnel on the Northern Line."

Jeremy smiled politely. "You need to be back at the *centre* of things, Phineas," he went on patiently. "Where all the right people are. Times are changing in publishing, old son, especially in crime, and you have to move with 'em—which is *precisely* what I did with my new leading character. And look how well that served me," he added, and, putting his sunglasses on again, leaned back with his wine.

"The new PI," Phineas said, to show interest.

Jeremy held up a finger.

"*Ah*, but he's not a PI. You have *read* my Gunter books?" he asked with quick suspicion.

"Yes. Yes, of course. I –"

"Ah. I see. So you assumed, then, that because my last lead was a PI, so was this one. Yes?" Jeremy waited with a small expectant smile.

"Well, yes ..." Phineas said cautiously. "Yes, I – er ..."

Jeremy slapped the white plastic table from the Patio Living department in one of Bryony Owen's catalogues. "And that's *precisely* the sort of thing I like to hear!"

"Is it?"

"I should say it is! Because it indicates, Phineas, that the *who* of Gunter is stronger than the what."

"Ah," Phineas said.

"You probably didn't even notice that Gunter carries neither a first name nor any sort of rank. Am I right?"

"Well, now you come to mention it, I – er –"

"Don't worry – you're not alone!" Jeremy said on a laugh. "No, it seems that as far as my readers are concerned there's only Gunter. Gunter and the dark dragons he must slay, the streets he must walk. There's no cosy backdrop of a home life for Gunter, Phineas. Only a lonely bed in a room that's more of a lair than a home. Gunter has no personal life, carries no baggage, has no past and is indifferent to the future. He is the *now*, Phineas. The immediate, happening present. He is Gunter."

"With a G," Phineas said, making a contribution.

Jeremy held up a warning finger. "Don't mistake me. He is no mere cipher. He is a man. Sometimes too much of one, too human. Indeed, one sometimes gets the impression that he bears the sins of the world. But he's a man stripped of almost all identity, except that needed to make his way among us, an existential, avenging angel in the gutters of the London night."

Jeremy stared off for a moment behind his sunglasses, the grimness of Gunter's existence etched into his face.

"Ah," Phineas said, and lifted the bottle again from the silver-plated wine cooler and stand from another of Bryony's catalogues -"Guaranteed to impress at dinner parties".

And when it was obvious that that was all he was going to say, Jeremy leaned back with his freshened glass and said, "Quite frankly, old chum, it's time the whole genre was moved on. Some of the stuff on the shelves today hasn't got much further than the body in the library."

Phineas stiffened. In his last Inspector MacNail book, *The Killer with Green Fingers,* the murdered body of an unknown man was discovered in an allotment shed, and in *Death Cashes a Cheque* a blonde in the same circumstances was found in a bathroom.

"Or perhaps an allotment shed or bathroom?" he suggested casually.

Jeremy, his train of thought interrupted, frowned. "What?"

"Never mind, Jeremy. It's of no importance," Phineas said, not without a certain sadness, seeing then what he'd long suspected. That his old friend Jeremy had probably never got much past his own name in the signed copies he sent him.

"There is no question, Phineas, that today's readers of crime fiction demand more. They are not only younger than in the past, they are also more cerebral. You take some of the work being done in America. Murder with the gloves off -"

"Nice title," Phineas murmured absently. And then, "Actually, Jeremy, the Americans quite like my work."

Well, at least one did. He was a great fan of MacNail. Although even Phineas would be pushed to call Humphrey cerebral.

"Yes, I'm sure they do," Jeremy said smoothly. "And anyway, that isn't a title. It's a description. Murder with the gloves off. Murder stripped of almost everything but the act itself. Murder most bloody indeed – but the colour of *real* blood, and deeds rich with psychological complexity. Murder for *today*, Phineas!"

"I think you'll find that Shakespeare got there before you."

"We are discussing modern crime fiction."

"Yes, well, I still think it would make a good title," Phineas said obstinately.

Jeremy sighed. "As a title, Phineas," he said heavily, "it would be a perfect illustration of what's wrong with the current state of much of the crime writing in this country. It's out of date, old fashioned. It's *cosy*," he finished brutally. "Now, compare it with the titles of my four Gunter novels. None of them has the word murder or death in them, do they?"

"No …" Phineas said, as if mentally running through them. "No, I can't say they do."

"Quite. Yet there are at least half a dozen murders in each book. And you take– and I say this as a friend, Phineas –you take your man, MacHale– "

"Nail," Phineas said evenly. "MacNail. Detective Inspector Murray MacNail. You have *read* my books, I take it, Jeremy?"

"Yes, yes, of course, I have. Slip of the tongue, that's all. But there you are, Phineas. I mean – MacNail …" Jeremy spread his hands, resting his case.

Phineas put his head back and regarded his friend from under the brim of his Gent's Superior Panama.

"And just *where* am I, exactly, Jeremy?"

"Well," Jeremy said with a laugh, "it's hardly stark realism, is it. I mean, come on – is anybody actually *called* Mac*Nail*?"

"Yes. MacNail is."

"You know perfectly well what I mean. But perhaps it's better if we dropped the subject."

"I wasn't the one who brought it up."

"Yes, well …"

Jeremy lifted his sunglasses to consult his watch. "The girls are taking their time."

"It might interest you to know, Jeremy," Phineas told him, "that an awful lot of people like MacNail– like reading about him. An awful lot of people."

Jeremy's expression challenged that.

"Yes, well, you'd have a lot more people reading you if you made your writing a bit more modern, a bit more with it. That's all I'm saying. Still, that's up to you." Jeremy checked his watch again. "Where *are* those women?"

Phineas put his head back again and studied him.

"You know, I think perhaps, Jeremy, you make the mistake of confusing quantity with quality."

Jeremy took his sunglasses off.

"Are you suggesting my work has no quality to it?"

The end of Phineas's cigarette went overboard.

"I am suggesting, Jeremy, that you should take a look at some of the company you're keeping, the quality of some of the work on that bestseller list you boasted of, before patronising others. That's all I meant." Phineas smiled at him. "Speaking as a friend, of course."

Jeremy shook his head. "Jealousy's a terrible thing."

Phineas laughed scornfully. "*What*? Jealous of that ..."

"Go on. Go on –say what you were going to say!"

"Well, all right. I'm not altogether sure *what* I was going to say. Only that whatever it was, it would have had the word pretentious in it."

"Pretentious?" Jeremy looked as if he'd been struck.

"Well," Phineas said lightly, "you did ask."

"I think, Phineas, that after that remark you and I have nothing more to say to each other. Now or at any time in the future. When Roz *does* get back we'll collect our things from the pub and be off."

"Suit yourself."

Phineas turned and stared out over the river. Jeremy put his glasses on again and drummed with his fingers on the table.

"Pretentious," he said then. He removed his glasses. "Pretentious," he said again, and gave a short laugh. "That word is the last refuge of the dim and the unimaginative. A play, a painting, a book – if they don't understand it, it's pretentious. An attitude which is, I have to say, fairly typical of this sort of reactionary backwater."

"Twaddle," Phineas, who'd been making a show of considering it, said. "Yes, that was the other word I'd have used. Twaddle. Pretentious twaddle."

Jeremy shot to his feet. "You'll take that back!"

"I don't think so."

Phineas kicked away his chair, and the two men stood facing each other. MacNail meets Gunter.

They were then saved from having to do anything more strenuous about it by the arrival of Sally and Roz, Jeremy's wife, back from a trip to the shop.

"Sorry we've been so long," Sally said cheerily. "I don't have to tell you we've been gabbing. Honestly – this place!"

The two men had dressed after swimming, but the women had simply put shirts on for the trip to the shop, Roz in the shirt she'd arrived in and Sally wearing one of Phineas's. And it occurred to him that while he might be streets behind in the book sales department, when it came to females in bikinis his won hands down. She'd caught the sun, her skin alive with it, her fair hair, dried after the river, shining the colour of straw. She wore a red gingham costume, which somehow suggested an innocence that was entirely at odds with the amount of flesh she had on show. Phineas groaned inwardly.

"You must have sent old Pugh the Pew's blood pressure shooting up, wandering in like that."

"We've got tops on," Roz said. She was looking from one man to the other.

"They've been having one of their silly arguments, Sally, I can tell. You've been having an argument, haven't you?"

Her husband removed his sunglasses again in a pained sort of way, and said in a reasonable man sort of voice, "No, we have not been arguing, Roz. Mr Cook does not argue, does not debate. Mr Cook takes the route of the intellectually lazy, or *inadequate*, and simply chucks insults about."

He smiled at his wife, sharing his amusement with her. "My work, you'll be interested to learn, darling, is, according to our Mr Cook here, so much pretentious nonsense."

"Twaddle. I said twaddle," Phineas put in. "For the record."

"I told you didn't I, Sally," Roz said with a laugh. "They've had one of their silly arguments."

Her husband put his glasses on again. "Therefore – and with apologies, of course, to the lovely Sally– I think you'll agree that we have no alternative but to leave forthwith."

Roz laughed again. "I don't agree any such thing. We've just bought lunch. With ice-cream. And anyway, I'm enjoying my-self if you're not. Come on, Sally, let's leave the silly little boys to it."

The two women made their way to the small kitchen in the stern, while the two men sat stiffly down again, and, folding their arms, looked away from each other.

Chapter Twenty-Seven

While the men waited frostily on deck for their lunch, the women were sitting at the kitchen table with a bottle of wine.

Roz had told Sally about Jeremy's affair with a girl from his publishers, and Sally told Roz about the woman Phineas had an affair with in Kingham.

"She's got a fish shop there."

"What? A wet fish shop? *Kinky!*"

"No, no, sorry, I meant fishing shop. You know, anglers."

"And is he still seeing her, the louse?"

"No, no, I'm sure he's not."

"Emm," Roz said doubtfully, and sniffed.

"He swore that it's finished – I know, I know. But I think this time he means it."

"Oh, Jerry *means* it – he meant it when he finished with a woman from a reading group he was seeing and then took up with a barmaid – and he meant it when he finished with the barmaid, exchanging her for the girl from his publishers," she said, which set Sally off about Phineas and Lucy the barmaid from the pub.

"They're all the same, Sally, men. Total arses. *Total* arses, the lot of 'em. Make him pay, darling. That's what I do. That charm bracelet you admired earlier is twenty-four carat. And I don't own a label now that isn't haute couture. If you stray, you pay, that's my motto."

"I'm not sure I could do that, Roz. And anyway, Phineas doesn't have the money," Sally said, and burped gently. "Oh, I beg your pardon."

"Granted," Roz said.

Sally solemnly inclined her head.

"Thank you, Roz. And I mean, it's not as if we're married or anything. It's different for us."

Roz looked appalled. "I don't suggest you go *that* far, darling. Not with a writer. For god's sake – don't even think of marrying a writer! They're even bigger arses. Absolute bloody *bas-tards*!"

She picked up the bottle and saw that it was empty.

"Oh, dear, we seem to have finished it. Now how did we do that?"

Sally looked at the wine rack. "Shall we?"

"And why not! He owes you that at least, darling, a few glasses of wine. And he's got enough there."

"He gets it from a discount shop across the border."

"I'll do the honours."

Roz pulled a bottle out of the rack, and then looked at the label. "Not that one, I don't think. That's not from a discount shop, across the border or anywhere else. It's a Château Mouton-Rothschild. Not that I know all that much about wine. But I do know that *that* is a very expensive one. Here we are, how about a nice medium dry Riesling? It's fruity, it says. I could do with a bit of fruity in my life just now.

"Cheers, darling," she said after pouring.

"Cheers, Roz. And I – well, I hope it works out for you."

"What? Me and the old man? Depends what you mean by works out, dear, I suppose. I'll stick with it for now, see what happens."

"Have you ever seen this girl at Jerry's publishers?"

Roz shook her head. "No. And I don't need to. She'll be blonde, and think he's wonderful, and be young enough to be his daughter. You know he wears a weave thing, do you? Oh yes!" she said, delighted to find that Sally didn't. "He didn't bring it with him because he knew we'd be swimming. But yes, he's got a sort of top piece, to lend body to what he's got left up there."

"Phineas is losing his as well. And he's getting a beer belly," Sally said, cheerfully disloyal.

"It looks ridiculous, Jerry's. All bouffant. Like a blow-waved hairy hamster. You can see it on the dust jackets of his Gunter books. Grinning away like a politician on them. Have you read any of Jerry's books?"

Sally looked embarrassed. "Well, no, actually, I – er –"

"Well, don't worry, darling – neither have I. Not his Gunter ones, anyway. Too gloomy for my taste. Give me a nice cosy village whodunit any day."

And Sally, who currently had an historical romance by her bed, confessed that she couldn't get along with Phineas's work either. And was about to add something about MacNail when the telephone in the sitting room directly opposite went.

It rang through to the outdoor extension bell rigged up on a corner of the sitting room roof, breaking the frigid silence on deck.

Phineas almost leapt to his feet in relief.

He grinned in at the two women, the doors of both rooms open in the heat, and went in to take the call.

It was Sarah. She had a new fishing client for Owain and couldn't get hold of him. Was he there? Phineas said he wasn't, and then, unable to resist a joke, no matter how weak, said that maybe he'd gone fishing, and laughed.

And Sally, about to say something to Roz, picked up that part of it.

She took a sharp breath. "That's what he used to say to that woman I told you about!" she hissed.

"The one with the fishing shop?"

"Yes. That was the code they used when the coast was clear," Sally said, as Phineas chatted blithely on. "He's probably arranging to see her now. In code. And *laughing* about it. The swine!"

Roz, her attention switching from Phineas back to Sally, couldn't resist asking how she knew about it.

"*She* boasted about it – the smelly old fish woman did. She told a friend, who told another friend, and that friend knew someone in the village here and told her, and she told Jasmine Roberts who lives on the next boat down, and told her not to say a word to anyone about it, she did, but Jasmine told Annie, you know, Annie Owen, and Annie told me," Sally went on, hearing in her own voice not only the gossipy tones of Batch Magna but also the rhythms of a border accent.

She was, she thought, not for the first time, steadily going native.

"It's this place. They've got nothing better to do here. Got sex on the brain, they have. *Sex* on the bloody brain!" she said, and laughed with abrupt shrillness.

"He's a total arse," she said, and burst into tears.

"*Shhh,*" Roz said, not unsympathetically. "I'm trying to listen."

Phineas, glancing idly across at them, saw Roz on the edge of her chair, one ear cocked intently in his direction, and Sally dabbing at her eyes with a dishcloth.

He told Sarah he had to go. He had, he said, something coming to the boil in the kitchen.

"What on *earth* is the matter?" he asked, standing in the kitchen doorway.

Roz shook her head at the sheer hypocrisy of the question. Sally ignored him.

And then she lifted her glass and made a face at the wine.

"Ugh! This is dis*gusting*. Nasty cheap stuff. Well, we know where that belongs, don't we?"

She stood, and picking up both glasses, tossed the contents into the sink. "Out you go! Don't want any nasty cheap stuff here – don't want any nasty *lying* cheap stuff here. And that," she added briskly, picking up the bottle. "Don't like the look of that, either. Got a boring label. *Bor-ing*," she said, pouring it down the sink.

Phineas watched as, humming unnervingly, she made a show of examining the contents of the wine rack.

"Oh, look!" she said, pulling one out. "That's a *much* prettier label."

Phineas saw the label himself then, just before she popped the cork.

"Sal – *ly*," he said weakly, and watched as she generously slurped Chateau Mouton-Rothschild 1957 into the two glasses.

"Sally! –" he started firmly.

"Cheers, Roz! Down the hatch!" she cried.

"Cheers, Darling!" Roz said, throwing it back with her.

"*Mmm* – lovely! We'll have some more of that," Sally said enthusiastically, lifting the bottle.

Phineas tried again. "Look here, Sally –"

"Oh! I've just remembered, darling!" she said to Roz. "What that shop's called we were talking about. The you-know-what shop. It's called –"

She leaned forward and whispered across the table.

"What?" Roz said on a laugh.

Sally looked disdainfully across at Phineas, an eavesdropper at the door, and leaning forward again put a hand up to her face to shield what she had to say.

"It's called –" Sally started. "It's called – " she said, before losing it again.

"What?" Roz said, laughing with her.

"It's called – it's called the Rising Fly! She sells tackle. Fishing tackle! For rising flies!" Sally got out, the explosions of laughter following Phineas back along the deck, propelled by the heat of indignation.

Why was it, he wanted to know – why *was* it, that whenever anything's wrong, he got the damn blasted blame for it? No matter what it's about – send for Phineas Cook! It seemed to be a local sport these days. And he was ruddy well sick up to here with it!

"Jeremy – Jeremy," he said without preamble, "I think we ought to resume relations long enough for me to tell you that unless we get it ourselves, we can forget about lunch. Those two are too busy getting sloshed back there."

"So that's what all the hilarity's about."

"It's Sally's doing. She's mad at me for something – but for the life of me I *can*not think what!"

Jeremy was immediately sympathetic. "Yes, awkward that, old chap. When one's no idea what sort of ball they're going to send down, how is one supposed to know how to play it?"

"I thought I was up to date with everything," Phineas muttered, frowning over it, more gales of laughter reaching them from the kitchen.

He looked at Jeremy. "That's a bottle of Chateau Mouton-Rothschild you're listening to. The fifty-seven. My one and only bottle."

"Mmm," Jeremy murmured appreciatively. "Not quite as good as the fifty-nine, but still ..."

"I bought it the very first week I arrived here. Everything was new then – including my DI, MacNail. It was to celebrate selling the first film option. That's why it was still sitting there." He shook his head. "I was a fool, I see that now. I *see* that now. Boy, do I see it!"

Jeremy came to a decision. He stood as if to attention.

"Phineas, I want to apologise unreservedly for my remarks. I had no right to take the attitude I took. To insist that one crime novel, merely by virtue of being different, is somehow superior to another. I'm afraid all this television nonsense rather went to my head. I just hope you feel able to accept it."

"Yes, yes, yes, old man, of course, I accept," Phineas said with a touch of impatience, busy with his thoughts.

And then he too seemed to come to a decision.

"But it's *I*, Jeremy, who should apologise to *you*. Because do you know what? Do you know what, Jeremy? You were right."

"Oh, I wouldn't –"

"No, you were right. My attitude was typical of this place, I see that now. *Typical*. Batch Magna all over. Narrow-minded. Insular. *Reactionary.*" He shook his head. "I just hadn't realised I was so far gone."

Jeremy looked appalled. "Phineas, I didn't mean – "

Phineas held up a hand. "No. No, Jeremy. You were right."

He smiled on his friend, the smile of someone who has gone ahead.

"Because a truth is unpalatable, Jeremy," he said gently, "doesn't make it any less true. You were right. And I'm grateful to you for it. Thank you, old chum. You've opened my eyes. I see now that the Cluny isn't the only backwater I'm stuck up. And it's ruddy well high time I did something about it!" he added with heat, looking about him as if wondering where to start, and then snorting derisively at what he saw.

"Jeremy – Jeremy, I feel like I've been asleep here all this time. But I'm awake now, all right. Boy, am I awake!"

"Phineas, look, I – "

"And do you know something?" Phineas said, turning his beatific smile in the direction of the kitchen and more laughter. "Do you know something, Jeremy? They are welcome to my one and only bottle of Château Mouton-Rothschild nineteen fifty-seven. Yes, Jeremy, welcome to it. Welcome to my future – a future which would otherwise be still sitting there twenty years from now. Because where I'm going, Jeremy, where I'm going, old man, there'll be plenty of corks popping, plenty of things to celebrate, I promise you. And I can't *wait* to get started. London – here I come!"

Jeremy looked uneasily at his friend.

This wasn't supposed to happen. They'd been exchanging banter about rural sloth versus the London rat race, and taking the odd potshot at each other's work, for years. They'd both got a bit huffy about it at times, but none of it was really meant. And they certainly weren't expected to actually *do* anything about it.

He knew, of course, what had changed things. And he knew he should have left well alone.

Because the brutal truth was that, whether here or in London, writing for the blood, guts and psychology end of the market, the end currently where the money was, Phineas was unlikely to get anywhere *near* the same sort of success. Simply because Phineas hadn't a Gunter in him.

Phineas was … well, Phineas was Phineas.

And he should have left well alone.

"Well, how about a bite to eat first, old chap?" he said carefully. "And as we're obviously not going to get the bib on here, suppose you let me stand you lunch at the pub, and we can talk about things there. How does that sound? Mmm?" he said soothingly, guiding his friend by his arm towards the gangway, while Phineas looked again at his world, and shook his head over what he saw there.

Dozing in the heat, Sikes opened one eye, considered it, and then closed it again.

Chapter Twenty-Eight

Phineas insisted on buying a bottle of fizz at lunch, making a start, as it were, on his new future, airily telling Patrick to put it on his slate.

And looking as if he had already arrived at that future, a cosmopolitan among the yokels, sitting back expansively with his champagne, a faint smile playing about his lips as Jeremy, with the air of a rather desperate second-hand car salesman, tried to sell him back Batch Magna, praising what, over the years of visiting Phineas, he had spent a good deal of time sniping at, while Phineas, humouring him, said, "Yes, yes, no doubt of it," and, "Oh, I quite agree," and, "Oh, yes, very pretty, and all that," and even added in a bored sort of way that he wouldn't mind considering the place for the odd weekend bolthole away from it all, if it wasn't so far from town –from where things were at. Which set him off again telling Jeremy what Jeremy, all these years, had been telling him, until Jeremy, hardly able to get a word in edgeways, finally gave up.

Smoking the cigars Phineas had also added to his slate, the two men wandered out onto the pub's terrace with their drinks after lunch, and found half of Batch Magna sitting out there. Or at least that part of it that, for Phineas, meant Batch Magna.

Phineas surveyed the scene, puffing complacently away.

He was, he supposed, going to miss the dear old things.

Still, broken eggs and omelettes and all that, the new Phineas thought with breezy callousness.

"No shirkers today, Commander, I see," he said. The Commander was sitting with Priny, a lunchtime pint of Black Boy in front of him, sending up contented signals of smoke from a briar, Stringbag the dog settled in under the table.

He glanced up in startled surprise, and then regarded him as if Phineas was the last person he expected to see there.

The Commander had been working in the wardroom, the old wheelhouse of the *Castle*, pursuing, under wall charts marked with brimming treasure chests and sprouting whales and cherubs with winds on their breath, fresh evidence of the location of lost Atlantis. Having spent the morning over charts illustrating isotherm and isoseismal patterns and the theory of continental drift, he had found to his great excitement and utter astonishment that he had landed up somewhere under the South China Sea. He had yet fully to come back from there.

"My dear fellow!" he said, beaming at him as if to make up for it. "Yes. Yes, indeed. Even Harriet mustered today. *And* on her second sherry. Not, of course, that I'm counting."

Miss Wyndham was sharing a table with Annie and Jasmine Roberts, Annie's eldest daughter, Bryony, and Humphrey's mom, Shelly, and Clem, the relish of a good gossip in the air.

Honestly! Phineas thought, this place.

Miss Wyndham was wearing a long-sleeved summer dress, a straw hat with a wide brim and a silk rose shading her face, an English lady keeping cool in a foreign heat. Bryony had her baby son on her lap, spooning him pureed fruit between sips of her wine. A couple more of her children, with some of Jasmine's and their friends, were chasing each other round the tables, and up and down to the river, scrambling over the upended mahogany sculling boats for hire beached on the slip below.

At another table Ffion and Daniel sat with a few friends from the village over pints of Sheepsnout.

He'd forgotten about Daniel.

Still, if his son wanted to come back next summer, which he very much doubted, then one of his friends, or the Owens, could put him up. So that was all right, the new Phineas thought casually.

"You remember Jeremy, Jeremy Bryant," he said to the Commander and Priny.

"Of course, of course – how are you, m'boy," the Commander said, fixing him with his good eye. In the other, haymakers toiled in miniature in a landscape by Henry Parker.

"Fine, sir, thank you. And you, Commander?"

"Oh, still afloat, you know, m'dear fellow, still afloat. A bit holed in parts and listing a little, it's true. But still afloat. Still afloat."

"And Priny," Jeremy went on, removing his yachting cap with a flourish, "looking, if I may say so, as young as yesterday and as lovely, as incomparably lovely, as ever."

"Darling!" Priny laughed throatily at the extravagance, the sound pure bottled nightclub, a large Plymouth gin in one hand, a cigarette in an amber holder in the other.

Her sun hat looked a vaguely nautical affair, in sugar-pink straw worn with Hollywood-sized sunglasses and a pink chiffon scarf holding it in place and tied under her chin. The rest of her was largely in red, a bullfighter print shirt and striped Capri pants with red deck shoes, her nail extensions crimson claws matching her lipstick.

Phineas, keeping his imminent departure from Batch Magna to himself for now, then took Jeremy across to where Humphrey was sitting with Tom Parr, listening agog to Tom talking about the days of the old CSC, when the paddlers puffed importantly up and down river, sounding their steam whistles as if to alert shipping.

To Humphrey, the thought of being at the wheel of one of them, pulling on a steam whistle, was even better than that of having Tower Bridge going up and down in the back garden.

Jeremy knew Tom, but hadn't yet met the new squire, in his Yankees baseball cap, grinning amiably at him above a shirt which looked how an explosion in a packed summer flowerbed might look.

"Humph– call me Humph," he said, cutting short Phineas's more formal introduction, and pumping Jeremy's hand, telling him that any friend of Phineas's was a friend of his, and what did he want to drink?

Jeremy, getting his hand back, insisted that he wanted to buy a drink.

He included Priny and the Commander in the round, and after being introduced to Humph's mom on his way to the bar, extended the invitation to Shelly and the rest of her table, even persuading Miss Wyndham to take another glass with him, while Shelly sat touching at her hair with its new colour job, strawberry blonde, and wondered if he was married. Phineas, with a pen and the back of an envelope Miss Wyndham dug out of her handbag, jotted down the orders on the back of it, following on behind when Jeremy then stopped to say hello to Daniel and Ffion, and Phineas added their drinks and those of their friends. While Jasmine, seeing where things were heading, shot off to fetch her guitar.

And a while later it was weekend business as usual on the river, when half the pub's terrace, and a good bit of the pub in bottles and cans, followed Phineas and Jeremy up the gangway of the *Belle* to continue the jolly, and on came Sally and Roz, who'd been diving off the starboard paddlebox, climbing back on deck up the ladder fixed to one side of it, squealing with laugher, and as carefree and as naked as water babies.

Chapter Twenty-Nine

Mrs Pugh, upstairs with the television, as it was half-day closing, knew what her husband was up to all right when he popped in with a pair of field glasses round his neck to tell her that he was off out for a while.

"Ornithological studies, you know, dear," he added, blinding her with science, and sucked in a superior sort of way on a tooth.

But Mrs Pugh knew what ornithological meant all right, she'd looked it up ages ago in the library in Kingham. And she knew also that the sort of birds her husband studied weren't the ones you put nuts out for in winter.

Mrs Pugh didn't mind, as long as he left her alone, and it was something else to pass on over the post office counter tomorrow morning.

"Have a nice time, Howell," she said, without taking her eyes off the screen.

Mr Pugh stole, furtive with lust, along the High Street and down into Upper Ham, led on by the image of the two women standing, as brazen as you like, in the shop earlier, licking at ice-creams in their bikinis.

In Upper Ham he headed straight for a gap in the break of bushes and trees which stood between the river and the lane. Mr Pugh had been there before.

And up this hawthorn on the river bank before, with one of its boughs, seven or eight feet up, reaching out over the water. Not ideal, but in his experience it was the best spot among the trees there from which to see but not be seen.

Mr Pugh, ardent birdwatcher, scrambled eagerly up it.

He made himself comfortable and trained the glasses on the *Belle*.

And almost dropped them.

"Sodom and Gomorra!" he breathed, unable to believe his luck. They were both naked. Not a stitch between them.

"They're naked, man! *Naked*," he told himself. "Naked and dripping."

One of them, the visitor, had her head back and was laughing wantonly, laughing and pushing her breasts out. Fresh from London and gagging for it already, she was. And the other, Phineas Cook's latest doxie, had her arms out and was moving her body, as if shaking it at the sun. Come and get it!

"Careful – careful," he muttered, with vague urgency, inching his way along to try for a better look.

"You will have scurvy and itch, boils and tumours," he muttered excitedly, trying to keep the glasses steady. "You will have madness, blindness, fear and panic. It is the word of God!" he promised, the Curses for Disobedience, which had followed him from a chapel childhood, following him now as he moved along the bough, lost to the heat of their eternal damnation, theirs and his, and to the sound of the wood creaking in protest under him.

The two women were still on deck when half of Batch Magna, or so it seemed to them, trooped up the gangway of the *Belle*. Phineas had time to note that he had not been wrong in his assessment that Sally had the better figure of the two, before they scrambled back up onto the paddlebox and jumped for it.

"What fun," Miss Wyndham said vaguely, unsure how she was supposed to take it.

Phineas peered over the side at the two heads bobbing about in the water.

"Would you like something to read while you're waiting? This is likely to go on for some time," he said, as Jasmine started tuning in her guitar. "All right, all right – no need to take that attitude. I'll put a couple of towels on the rail here. And then perhaps you'd get dressed before joining us. This is a respectable gathering, this is."

While they waited, studiously looking elsewhere, for the two women to climb back up, the Commander wandered down to the bow.

He was leaning on the rail there, a pipe on, gazing idly out, when he caught a movement downriver, on the bank between the *Belle* and Jasmine's boat, the *Cluny Queen*.

There was someone up a tree there, perched on a bough.

The Commander trained his good eye on the figure. It was a man, he decided, as with a crack like a pistol shot the bough snapped and the person dropped with a yell into the river.

The Commander took his pipe from his mouth.

"Extraordinary," he muttered.

He watched with interest as a head bobbed to the surface, and there was a great deal of frantic thrashing about.

All the fellow had to do, the Commander could have told him, was to find his feet and walk in. No, belay that – on second thoughts, trudge in. And carefully, come to think of it, he remembered. The riverbed there was cratered with pockets of deep silt.

He saw that the man, whoever he was, had just found that out, disappearing from view, and then popping up and disappearing again, several times, before crawling, shedding mud and water, up onto the bank.

"Extraordinary," the Commander said again, his attention caught then by the popping of a cork. Normal service on the *Belle* had been resumed.

Not as far as Sally was concerned it hadn't. As far as Sally was concerned all services were now off. As she was. Just as soon as she had finished dressing. And she would not be coming back. She should have done it long ago.

Phineas was waiting for her when she came out of the saloon with Roz, looking for all the world as if nothing had gone on – or as if he thought he'd got clean away with it, more like. And then, when he saw her face, she got his puzzled, little boy hurt look. What sort of fool did he take her for!

Roz walked past him with her head in the air.

Sally didn't. Sally marched straight up to him.

Phineas took a couple of steps back.

Sally narrowed her eyes at him, and was about to give him both barrels, all the words she'd rehearsed furiously while dressing, when Anne Owen, who'd stopped off first at the *Felicity H* to pick up a contribution of her home-made wine, came up the gangway armed with bottles and with Owain in tow.

"Look what I found at home," she said.

"Ah, Owain! Did Sarah manage to contact you?" Phineas greeted him with relief, glad of a chance to delay whatever it was Sally had to say –because whatever she had to say, he just *knew* he wasn't going to like it. He wondered what she, and a few others he could name, would do when he had gone, who they would find to carry the can for things then.

"Howdo, Phineas. Yes, yes, she did, thanks."

"Only she rang here earlier looking for you."

"Yes, I was out, like," Owain said absently, grinning at the fun bubbling away on deck, and the sound of Jasmine singing.

"That fishing client she'd lined up sounds jolly good – important businessman, prominent member of the local Chamber of Trade, or whatever it's called," Phineas burbled on, hoping to prolong things. "Never can tell where that might lead. Before you know it you've got the entire Chamber of Whatnot queuing up for your services. Why, I wouldn't be surprised if ..."

Phineas trailed off, as Owain, no longer listening, and with the light of a jolly in his eye, followed his wife and the rest of the bottles to join the others.

Phineas turned to face Sally, and whatever she had waiting for him.

And, startled, took another step back.

She was smiling at him. Sally was smiling at him. A smile of unnerving tenderness, her eyes quite misty with it.

He flinched as she reached up, and hooking in a finger into the open neck of his shirt, pulled him to her and kissed him, full on the lips.

And then put her cheek to his. "*Later*," she promised, breathing it in his ear, before adding, quite matter-of-factly, that she must go and tell Roz something.

Phineas watched her go with his mouth open.

He would never – never *ever*, no matter how long he lived, or how wise he might become, understand women.

They stood together at the rail of the *Belle* at the end of the day, unspeaking and content, the jolly long over, and Daniel out with Ffion in the Frogeye, the old car that Phineas had said he couldn't *wait* to turn in for a spanking new model, one with tinted, electronic windows, or whatever they were called, and a top speed of whatever it was Jeremy had said.

A white mist rolled off the water meadows and seeped like smoke along the river as dusk fell, and the rooks settled in the tops of the big sycamores in Mawr Wood. Above the darkening hills of the valley, the evening star flickered into life in a blue-green sky, pale with summer, and the owls started calling.

He hadn't meant it, of course. It was true he'd gone at it a bit this time, chucking everything overboard, firing not only Batch Magna but giving MacNail his cards as well – old MacTartan Slippers, as he'd slightingly and disloyally called him – and getting a newer, psychological model, and splashing a lot more gore about, and all that sort of thing. But he hadn't actually *meant* it. Of course, he hadn't. It had been the river talking, that's all.

He'd phone Jeremy at home tomorrow and tell him. He'll understand. He'll no doubt be a bit short about it, having gone to all that trouble to get him moving again, but he'll understand. Good old Jerry.

It had just been the river talking, that's all. It did that to people sometimes. You could get in a frightful lather about all *sorts* of things, just sitting on a river. You could put the world to rights and change your own life, or somebody else's, several times, all before breakfast. You could be as decisive and dynamic as you liked on a river – without actually having to *do* anything about it.

And *that*, as he'd had occasion many times in the past to point out, to himself as well as others, sparing no one, was precisely what was wrong with living on the thing, instead of somewhere more sensible, with one's feet firmly planted on the ground.

And he knew again that which he had never stopped knowing.

That he simply could not imagine living anywhere else – couldn't imagine why anyone would *want* to live anywhere else – but here, in this place.

"Bugger where things are at," he said, and laughed, suddenly, at nothing and at everything.

Sally stirred next to him. "Mmm, darling?" she murmured.

"I said, guggerderfinstadat. Which, my girl, is a local charm of great antiquity for luring unsuspecting females to one's bed."

"Well, darling, I don't normally believe in charms and all that sort of thing. But I have to say," Sally said a few minutes later, as Phineas closed the bedroom door behind them, "that this one certainly seems to be working."

Chapter Thirty

A week later, the story of the cooling of Mr Pugh's ardour has gone round the village and beyond –Mrs Pugh had seen to that – and Clem finally had to tell Sarah that the Hawis Stone had been stolen.

She'd reported it to the police on the day of the robbery and told Humphrey when she got home. And when she brought up the family legend attached to the loss of the Stone, Humphrey didn't joke about it this time. And even when he said it was a load of horse feathers he did so quietly, as if he might be over-heard, as if there were someone else in the Hall, apart at that time from them.

And then they had waited, hoping that it would somehow just turn up.

And when it didn't she phoned Sarah and told her, and Sarah didn't make any jokes about the curse, either.

Clem asked her to keep it to herself for now. And then she had to tell Shelly, who'd been doing a bit of dusting in the hall, near the phone, going over the same spot several times, and was agog to learn what Sarah had to keep to herself.

Clem told her and swore her to secrecy. And Shelly, later on that morning, meeting Annie on the way to the shop, swore her to secrecy, as well, because she just *had* to tell someone.

And by the end of the second day almost the entire village had been sworn to secrecy. Something else Mrs Pugh had made sure of.

And on the third day, the first of the sick pheasant poults was found.

Sion was whistling carelessly at his work, on his way to the coverts, a hundredweight of corn on one shoulder.

The sun had started to climb above the hills, its light firing the fields of dew before it as he drove up from the Keeper's Cottage, reaching with long smoky fingers deep into Cutterbach Wood, the air there drenched with birdsong singing on into it.

Not that Sion noticed. He was busy with thoughts of another kind of nature. He'd met her last night, at an away darts match in Llandos. A bottle blonde with the bedroom in her eyes and a back of the chapel laugh. A loose woman, that one – *defi*nitely, he promised himself, thinking about their date that night.

He shifted the weight of the sack on his shoulder and started up a game trail towards the coverts.

He was relieved to find, as he was each morning, that there had been no successful overnight visitors, the bottom of the perimeter netting on the two big release pens still firmly pegged down. He'd seen before where attempts had been made to get in, and had smelt dog fox around the pens. It was his constant concern that one would break in under the netting and wipe out most, if not all, of the stock.

The estate had dug deep into its meagre pockets to buy the chicks and would not be able to afford to do so again this year.

They had been brought in at six weeks, and now, three months on, their clipped wing feathers re-grown, they were able to fly over the netting. Sion had cut feed rides through the trees to encourage them to spread to higher and higher ground, up to where they'd be flushed from in the autumn, giving the guns good, high-flying sport.

He emptied the sack into a grain bin, and then whistling up the birds, started to scatter corn from a canvas shoulder bag along the rides, strewn with straw to give them something to scratch about in.

It was then that he spotted the sick poult. He'd lost a few to owls or jackdaws, who both killed for the eyes and brain, but not one yet to sickness.

It was standing, hunched, on its own, its feathers fluffed out and its eyes half-closed. He only knew one treatment for that, whatever ailed it.

He picked up the bird, took its head between thumb and index finger, and with one quick, strong movement crushed it, killing it instantly. He'd take it down later to the *Felicity H*, a potential source of maggots for fishing bait. Waste not, want not, as Annie says.

Later that morning, when he took water up to the coverts, he found another sick bird. And by the time he'd finished topping up the drinkers, two more had fallen ill.

"I just hope it's not a bloody epidemic of some kind," he said to Owain, going straight there after he'd finished doing the water.

Owain, who hadn't been up to the coverts since the spring, when he'd helped his son patch up the two old pens, pens that he himself had built many years before, asked about symptoms.

"Oh, I don't know, Da," Sion said, shrugging. "They just looked sick. You know? As if they had the flu, or something, like. Hunched up, with their feathers all fluffed out."

"Parasites, maybe. Often is with poults."

Owain then suggested mixing wormer in with their feed, and asked his son if he'd been cleaning the ground regularly. Sion said indignantly that, of course, he had.

And then Sion remembered something else.

"Oh, yes, and their breathing – they seemed to have trouble getting their breath, like, you know?"

Owain thought about it – but not for long.

"Hey! Hey, you ain't been spraying DDT or anything like that about, have you? Well, it's been done before," he said, when his son wanted to know what he took him for.

Owain pulled a turnip watch from a pocket of his green cord waistcoat.

"I've got a client due soon, but I'll come up later this afternoon if you like, and take a look."

But by that afternoon, Owain, a man with myth and legend bred into his border Welsh bones, knew there was no point. Because he knew then that it was not only the pheasants that were done for – their world was finished along with them. Of that he had no doubt.

He had been waiting for disaster in one form or another since learning of the loss of the Hawis Stone. He'd half-wondered about it, vaguely uneasy, when Sion told him about the poults. And by that afternoon he knew. And he knew there was no point trying to do anything about it because there was nothing that *could* be done about it.

There wouldn't be any happy ending this time, and he didn't care what anyone said. Because this time it was fate. A fate sealed the moment the Hawis Stone left the possession of the Strange family.

Owain even knew by then the name of the man who would do for their world, who would change everything, because that's what people, strangers, did. The man who would buy the estate when Humphrey and Clem finally saw that it was no good, that they had no choice but to sell.

He was the client he was due to take out on the river that morning.

His name was Marriott, a Midlands businessman –or entrepreneur, as he preferred to be called. "A man prepared to back his judgment on anything he thinks has pp written on it. Potential profit," Mr Marriott explained. "You can't expect to accumulate if you're not prepared to speculate."

"Oh, ah," Owain agreed.

"Well, I mean, it's only sound business sense. You take me, for example. A map of my business interests would fill up half a wall in any boardroom. Multi-investment, diversification, that's where the money is these days, Mr Owen."

"Oh, ah," Owain said again, and wondered where all the fish had gone.

They'd been out there on the punt for over thirty minutes now and he had yet to even see one. And the day had turned unexpectedly overcast, drawing warmth from the water. Afterwards, of course, as far as Owain was concerned, when he knew all that the morning had to tell him, it was just what he would have expected on such a day – a sky that threatened much more than rain.

He was about to suggest to his client that he might like to shut up, so that they could get a bit of fishing in, when Mr Marriott produced a half-bottle size hipflask and politely offered it to him first. And Owain immediately took the view that, as they were sitting there on his client's money, what the client did with the time was entirely up to the client.

"Good sport to you, sir!" Owain wished him cheerfully, and took a swig, the day suddenly warmed with the fire of a good single malt.

"Property," Mr Marriott said then, taking his turn with the flask. "That's the thing to get in on at the moment, Mr Owen. Plenty of pp in that, I can tell you, the way the market is these days. And as you might expect, I've been doing a bit of dabbling there myself. Getting a nice little portfolio together, ready for when prices go up again. It's not just knowing when to buy

–but more important, knowing when to *sell*. That's where the judgment comes in."

"Oh, you're right there, sir," Owain agreed, lifting the flask.

"Now you take that manor house of yours, Batch Hall, and its land. Well, it's all been let go, anyone can see that. Like a lot of these old families today, they obviously just don't have the money anymore."

"That's true," Owain said feelingly.

"Matter of fact," Mr Marriott said, glancing at him, "I've got my eye on the place myself. Already made an approach, in fact. You know, testing the water, like. Now, don't get me wrong," he went on, seeing that he had Owain's sudden, frowning attention. "Any offer I might make would be a fair one –more than fair. I wouldn't take advantage. I'm a traditionalist, me. I don't like to see these old county families go to the wall. But, well, I have to say," he added with a chuckle, "that I like the idea of passing up a good bit of pp even less. And there's plenty of that waiting there, I can tell you, for someone with a bit of cash to put in, and the right ideas. Hey!" he said a few moments later, Owain still busy taking in what he'd just heard. "What's happened to the fish today?"

Owain was about to tell him that his nattering had probably scared them off, and to probe him about the business with the Hall, when he spotted the first one of the morning.

It was a perch. Its silvery cream belly some ten yards or so off, being borne gently downstream, floating past them on its back.

Chapter Thirty-One

More fish were spotted over the following days, belly up, and more young pheasants found dead or dying, of course, there were, Owain could have told them that. He told Annie it enough times, intoning it like doom from the bed he'd taken to and refused to leave. This time, they'll have to bloody well carry him off the river.

He knew it wouldn't last, the reprieve they'd been given when sent from there last year. He just knew it. He'd said as much at the time, when back on the *Felicity H,* back with home, with the river, under their feet again, as Annie had put it, and everybody cheerfully unpacking, and telling each other how wonderful it was to be back, and how they just couldn't believe it.

It won't last, you know, he'd warned them, not bothering to take his coat off.

And he'd been right.

And even when Annie had later hotfooted it home with the news that a sample of river water had been found to contain high levels of organic waste, which had drastically reduced the oxygen content in the river, killing off the fish, and on another occasion that tests had established that DDT *had* been sprayed or poured over the ground in the coverts, the earth found to be soaked with it, as far as he was concerned he was still right.

So what? he replied, hardly bothering to lift his head from the pillow to do so. What does it matter how a curse worked? All that matters is that it does, he said, and wouldn't budge, even when the Commander came round to tell him the good news about the otter.

There had been no sign of the animals, the female and her three cubs in the den she'd made for them in a bank on Snails Eye, burrowed in under the spreading roots of an ash, since the river had gone bad. The Commander had kept regular watch with the glasses, and had then rowed over there, half dreading what he might find.

And when he found neither dead nor dying animals, he couldn't be sure what it meant. Whether they were battened down deep in their holt, or had escaped at the first taste of the water, or whether they'd died in it, of it, and their bodies carried downstream with the fish.

As he'd said to Priny, his hope was that, being an extremely bright sort of animal, which, of course, all otters were, and being, in the way of that animal, a good, sensible mother, she had crossed to the far bank and moved her family upriver by land, beyond the point where whatever it was had entered the water.

And then, that morning, out of habit and a little wistfully, he had lifted the glasses again to the island, and immediately brought her into view.

She was on her own, standing, sleek with the water she must have crossed to get there, on a bank above a mud slide, upright and quite still, and seeming to be gazing steadily at him.

He dared not breathe for a moment, and then he blinked and she was gone, as if she had never been.

Which Owain, not without sympathy, and while having no trouble in believing, as his friend did, that the animal was the recycled soul of the late and much-loved general, told him now what he thought was probably the case.

"You wanted to see her, so you saw her, imagined her, like, or it was a different animal, or something," he said, weary with melancholy.

"No, no, no." The Commander impatiently waved it away. "I didn't imagine her, nothing of the sort. And it was the same animal. I'd know those whiskers anywhere. She was staring *straight* at me, Owain. In the forthright sort of way he had, you know? Oh, it was the general all right. No doubt on it."

The Commander had first sighted the otter on the island last year, after more than a ten-year absence of such creatures on the home stretch of the river, and when it was thought the enemy stood at the gates, in a Hawaiian shirt.

Other people, the sort for whom two and two will *always* make four, no matter how many times they add them up, would no doubt have said it was simply coincidence that the animal, the same animal which featured on the Strange family crest, should have suddenly appeared after such a long absence, so soon after the death of the general and a time of threat to all he had held dear.

But when the Commander, a man who knew there was often nothing simple about coincidence, was doing the arithmetic it added up to far more than that, as he had lost no time in telling Owain.

And then the otter went missing.

It was later known that she was in cub and had been trapped by a water bailiff upriver at Horton Cross. He intended releasing the animal with her unborn young up on the Severn, well away from his beat. But she had then escaped, from a seemingly escape-proof pen, simply because, as Owain, who had been brought up on the magical powers of otters, had said, it was time to do so.

She wanted her cubs to be born in the den she'd made for them on Snails Eye. She wanted to bring them home.

And on one bright morning after, as it were, the skies above Batch Magna had cleared, when the enemy in a shirt found that, after all, he was a friend, the Commander on one of his regular sweeps of the island with the glasses had seen her again, and with her cubs this time, playing, carelessly, with them, as if to say, I told you so.

They were up and down on the mudslide, chasing each other, wrestling, somersaulting, diving for stones, and sending up bubbles from their other element below, as fleet there as fishes. Free of everything, even time, chucking it about as if there were no tomorrow. Which for them, of course, he knew there wasn't – not yesterday, or last week, or this year or the next. They cannot know time as we know time, and so are free of it.

It was a theory of the Commander's that time for farm animals scarcely moves from one day's grazing to the next. That were it to be represented on a clock face, it would be seen that in the evening the minute hand would scarcely have moved from where it was in the morning. While time for wild animals, on the other hand, was almost *constantly* on the go. Here and there, this way and that, leading them by the nose as well as the belly. And when they are not eating, or questing, or squabbling, or engaged in sundry other matters, they are playing. And then they are lordly, lords of time, with fields and rivers and seas of time, and all the skies to play in.

Time for us humans, as he had become increasingly aware, was a poor shackled thing in comparison. We are tied to it from birth, and burdened with its future as well as its past. The baggage of our lives and our fears of what might be. And the usual spree of youth aside, spend it with an eye on one sort of clock or another.

And watching their heedless play, on land and in the water, which, of course, was all the same to them, he could quite see why, the armorial connection aside, the general had returned in that form. And he decided that after coming back first as a water vole, and then as a buzzard, he would reserve a third tour as a river otter, with a fine set of whiskers.

"And she's here again, Owain," he went on, his good eye vivid with it. "Her cubs safe upstream somewhere, she's risked death to cross to the island to let us know that it's all right. To tell us to be of good heart, all will be well. As it was the last time. You'll see." The Commander spoke soothingly, coaxingly to him.

"So, put your trousers on, there's a good fellow," he went on briskly. "I've signalled everyone else, and we're all going to the pub to lift a glass or so to this most extraordinarily welcome news," he told him, which was stretching things a bit.

For a start, Annie had gone off to see her daughter, Bryony, to talk to somebody sensible for a change, she'd told Owain, like her one-year-old grandson. It was true that Phineas had agreed, but then Phineas didn't need a supernatural otter, nor indeed any other sort of animal, nor indeed any excuse of any sort, to turn out for a drink. The Commander hadn't been able to raise the Hall when he'd phoned, and Jasmine, trying, he suspected, to get one up on his otter, had said thanks very much, but it was old news. Her spirit cat had told her only yesterday that things would be all right, she'd just forgotten to mention it, that's all, and anyway she had shopping to do. And when he told Priny, she wanted to know if he'd been out in the sun again without a hat.

"I wouldn't be at all surprised," the Commander went on, "if it didn't go and end in a jolly. Wouldn't be at all surprised. So don't say I didn't warn you, Owain," he added enticingly.

But Owain was beyond even that.

He looked at his friend, his Welsh-dark eyes caves of deep, unreachable misery.

"It's no good, Commander," he said, as if summoning up the last of his strength to do so. "Even if it was the same animal, even if it *was* the general, there's nothing he could do about it. It's different this time. This time it's fate. *Ffawd*. And there's nothing anybody can do about that, in this world or anywhere else."

Chapter Thirty-Two

Except to hold another meeting in the kitchen of the Hall.
Because then at least it felt as if they were doing *something*
about it – if only to tell each other again that they didn't see
what they *could* do about it.

And now, at this latest gathering, they weren't even saying
that. They weren't saying anything.

Sion, slumped in his chair at the kitchen table, broke the
silence.

"I'd give a lot to know where they live," he said, more to
himself.

"We can't be sure it was them, Sion," Clem said reasonably,
referring to the badger baiters in Cutterbach Wood.

"Of course, it was them, honey – who else?" Humphrey said,
spreading his hands in appeal.

"Well, even if it was them, knowing where they live wouldn't
help the situation, would it?" Sarah sensibly pointed out.

"It would help me," Sion said grimly.

He looked at the others. "We're finished up there. And on
the river. The poults are almost completely wiped out. And
even if we had the money to restock we couldn't bring 'em on
in time. And as far as the river goes – well, if there's any fish left,
then we ain't seen them."

"We've still got the turkeys," Shelly said cheerfully, giving the word a South Bronx spin. "At least we'll eat well at Thanksgiving and Christmas. Yeah, well," she went on, when the others only smiled politely, "you did what you could, Sion - you both did. At least you can tell yourselves that."

Sion and Humphrey had cleaned away the grass and topsoil in the pens and feed rides, and put fresh straw down twice a day.

"I reckon it's the earth worms," Sion said. "I reckon it soaked down to them and when they come up, the birds eat 'em. Which just goes to show how much the bastards put down." Sion put a polite hand up to another yawn. He'd been sitting up all night again in the coverts with a 12-bore, just in case.

Sarah broke the silence this time.

"I take it that you're still against selling the Masters' Cottages?" she said carefully, referring to the four, habitable cottages on the river, built for the Masters of the CSC.

Clem sighed. "We've gone through all this, Sarah. They're estate *pensioners*. Without a pension. It's the least the estate can do."

"Yeah!" Shelly joined in. "You can't throw old Mrs Tranter and her husband out on the street. And Mrs Parks is nearly a hundred." Mrs Parks, who played bingo with Shelly, had started work at the Hall at fourteen and was a great source of upstairs, downstairs stories.

"And what about old Tom, and the kids, Will and Sandra, with their toddler?" Shelly went on indignantly.

"Nobody's getting thrown out of nowhere, Mom," Humphrey told her.

"Because as I've said," Sarah continued evenly, "that's the most obvious solution. Take out a bank loan to renovate them, and then put them on the open market. Riverside properties are highly desirable," she added temptingly.

Humphrey was shaking his head. "No way – no *way*! That was last year, throwing old people out on the street. They're staying where they are. Curse or no goddam curse."

"We have an obligation to them, to the pensioners. And Sandra and Will are village people," Clem added. "You understand that, Sarah."

Sarah blew out smoke from her roll-up. "Yes. Yes, of course, I do, Clem. And I rather thought you'd still see it that way," she said, her voice softening. "But, well, it doesn't leave us an awful lot to play with, does it? Those dwellings, along with the Keeper's Cottage, now comprise the estate's entire housing stock. Apart, that is, from the houseboats. And – "

"Hey! That's an idea. Sell the cottage," Sion put in. "I could get a –"

"No, no, no," Humphrey said, waving a meaty hand at him. "We're not selling the Masters' Cottages or the Keeper's Cottage, or the goddam houseboats. And anyway, we get rent from the paddlers."

"You get rent from two of them," Sarah pointed out. "The Cunninghams own theirs, and Annie and Owain are both estate pensioners."

"All right, all right – well, we get rent from two of them, then," Humphrey said shortly.

Sarah, who kept the books, added, "When, that is, they get round to paying it. Phineas is a month behind again, and when last I looked Jasmine owed three months' rent."

"Yes, well, she's had a few problems lately," Clem said.

"And Phineas is waiting on a royalty cheque," Humphrey muttered. "He's expecting one any day now," he said, sharing the news with the others.

"Well, there's no longer anything of value in the house," Sarah went on relentlessly. "All that went under the hammer yonks ago. You could always sell what's left of the estate. But then what's left of the estate means the land needed for fishing and shooting – the only real means you have of generating income. It's what I believe is called a Catch Twenty-Two situation. Shelly's Conies, and opening the house – that part of it, at any rate, that doesn't leak – to the public, and all the other, wholly admirable attempts to keep afloat won't do it, I'm afraid. Anywhere near."

When no one had anything to add to that, Sarah went on, "I think we've been putting this off rather. Understandably. And I hate to say it – hate to *have* to say it. But, well, looking squarely at the situation, as we must, I think we have to consider Mr Marriott's offer."

It took a few moments for Humphrey to take that in.

"What – selling up, d'you mean?"

"Yes, I do mean that. I'm sorry, but there it is. That's the reality, I'm afraid."

"We could get a loan on the Hall," Clem said, without much conviction.

"Of course, you could," Sarah agreed. "And risk losing it when you fail to make the repayments. And meanwhile he would have gone elsewhere. But that must be your decision."

"What, all of it? Would we have to sell all of it?" Humphrey looked shocked.

"Well, as far as Mr Marriott's offer is concerned, yes. The Hall and all available land in one packet. It's a prerequisite."

"Well, what does he want it for?" he asked, looking suspiciously at her.

"That I don't know."

"Probably wants to turn it into an hotel," he answered himself miserably.

"Now," Sarah cut in briskly, sitting on any untidy emotion before it could get going, "I've done some phoning around, canvassing several independent opinions from estate agents in both Church Myddle and Kingham, and I am assured that the offer made is, as was said, well above current market value. And that is the crux of the matter. That is the thing you should bear in mind when coming to a decision."

When nobody had anything to say to that, Sarah went on, "Before coming here this morning, I also rang the solicitors Mr Marriott engaged in Kingham. The offer is sound, but it does depend on the sale going through as expeditiously as possible."

"What's that supposed to mean?" Humphrey asked sulkily.

Sarah stubbed the last of her cigarette out in the ashtray. "In our case it means he wants vacant possession by early September."

"Blimey!" Shelly said, using an expression picked up from Mrs Parks.

"He don't mess about, does he?" Sion said.

"I really can't see you getting a better offer, or anywhere near. Especially not in the current market," Sarah added, not without sympathy. "And the Hall will get the attention it needs, inside and out. And its gardens, and maybe even its lodge, restored. It's how a lot of old houses survive these days. But, as I say, it must be your decision."

"Take up his offer and move into the Keeper's Cottage," Sion said pragmatically. "That's what I'd do. It's got two bedrooms. One of them don't even leak," he added, with a laugh.

Despite his woes, Humphrey couldn't resist asking where, in that case, Sion would sleep, if not in the bedroom that didn't leak?

"Oh, I wouldn't be there, in the cottage. I wouldn't stay on if you're selling. Wouldn't be right. Not without paying rent, it wouldn't."

"You're staying on and you're not paying rent!" Humphrey growled, taking the situation out on somebody. "I'm your boss, you'll do as you're goddam told!"

Sion laughed. "Not no more you wouldn't be."

"If you sell to Mr Marriott you could *buy* a house. Buy a couple of houses. Outright," Sarah put in. "In fact, there's one coming up shortly in the village. Anne Banks, who died recently, her husband, now he's getting on a bit, wants to move

187

into sheltered accommodation in Kingham. There's no family to leave it to, so he's selling. Which means, of course, that he must offer it to you, the estate, first," Sarah went on, referring to the late general's housing scheme which allowed local people to buy estate houses at well below market value, with a legal tie that, if they sold, they must sell back to the estate.

The estate no longer had the money to buy any of its stock back and now acted simply as agents, offering it first to any villager who might be interested, before releasing it to be sold on the open market. But for generations it had kept house prices down and a community together.

"It's detached, centrally heated, with three bedrooms – none of which I'm sure leaks – dining room, sitting room, and kitchen with all mod cons. They had a new one fitted only a few years back, apparently. It has a garage to one side of the property, a nice gravel drive, and well maintained front and back gardens."

Sarah smiled her estate agent's smile at them and waited.

"And we couldn't keep the peacocks," was all Clem said, more to herself, adding that small loss to the rest of it – reducing the rest of it to that small loss. "Not with neighbours, and the din the birds make."

"And you'd still have a very healthy balance sitting in the bank," Sarah said brightly. "There should even be enough to buy Shelly a small one-bedroomed flat, if that's what she wanted. Be a sound investment, too."

"Hey! C'mon – I couldn't take something like that. I'll be all right. I'll get a job and –"

"You *will* take it, Moms!" Humphrey told her.

"Oh, yes, you must," Clem agreed immediately. Shelly in the Hall was one thing, Shelly in a normal-sized house was quite another.

"So – is it settled then?" Sarah asked cautiously.

"So, we're not gonna endure then, after all," Humphrey said quietly.

Beati Qui Durant – 'Blessed are those who endure'. The Strange family motto, their coat-of-arms a castle with a lion and otter rampant.

Sarah studied her cousin for a few moments, and then said, "Humphrey, I'm going to tell you something I should have told you before now. I think you thought that I resented you here, resented that you were the one who had inherited. Is that not so?"

"Well, yeah – yeah, now you come to mention it, coz, I did think that," Humphrey said with a laugh, admitting it now, feeling free to admit it now.

The woman had unnerved him the first time he'd met her, with that accent and pedigree. She made him feel awkward, ungainly, a large clumsy colonial among fine, Old World furniture, stuff that had always been there.

But above all, she made him feel like an interloper, a usurper. It was, everyone seemed to agree, Sarah, the general's favourite granddaughter, who should have inherited.

"Yes, I thought so," Sarah said. "And purely out of an old woman's perversity, I allowed you to go on thinking that. And it was wrong of me. Because it isn't – and wasn't – true. In fact, Humphrey, I was relieved that I *hadn't* inherited."

The general hadn't discussed it with her, that hadn't been his way, and when she was told that the estate had passed to a distant cousin, an American, her feelings had been complex and mixed. Feelings that went back to the roots of her family in this place. But chief among them, after a first, quite illogical, reaction of disappointment and loss, had been relief.

Relief that she didn't have to carry the burden of it all. And that she wouldn't have to sell Batch Hall to meet that burden.

"You've fought well for it," she told them, "for the Hall, for the Strange family's place here. And now you have the burden of having to decide to sell. I'm just grateful that that decision isn't mine to have to make."

Humphrey, his mouth open at Sarah's disclosure, started when Clem reached across and put a hand on his.

"Darling, I really don't see what else we can do. Where else we can go from here. And, well, on a mercenary note, we at least know we'll be getting a good price ..."

Humphrey looked from Clem to the others, looked trapped.

"Well, he can't have the houseboats," he said with sudden heat. "He can have the fishing but not the paddlers. And he don't get the Keeper's and Masters' Cottages, neither. You can tell him that!"

Clem put a hand on his again.

Humphrey looked at Sarah.

"So, what do we have to do, then?" he asked quietly. "Ring him, or –"

"I'll do it, I'll deal with it," Sarah said quickly, being kind – I'll do it, you don't have to look.

So that was it, then. That's what that last silence between them in that kitchen said.

So that was it.

That was how over four hundred years of family history ended.

What border wars and the forces of Cromwell, the devastations of agricultural depressions, ruined harvests, foot and mouth and sheep rot, taxes and death duties, the late general and his sporting largesse, and Humphrey in his red Wall Street suspenders had failed to do, the loss of the Hawis Stone, as Owain from the depths of his wretched bed had been telling them all along, looked set to.

And then Miss Wyndham rode to the rescue on the 49 bus.

Chapter Thirty-Three

Miss Wyndham took the bus, which picked up in Batch Magna on Tuesday, Thursday and Saturday mornings, to Kingham, to visit the opticians there, among other errands she had in mind.

She had caught the cord of her reading glasses on a handlebar of her bicycle, and had broken one of the arms and popped a lens. It was a matter of pride with her that, at her age, she didn't need spectacles for everyday use. She seemed, as it were, to drop more stitches by the day when it came to her memory, but there was nothing wrong with her eyesight.

Except that she *did* need glasses for reading, and found their loss frustrating.

For one thing, she hadn't finished the half dozen American pulp fiction paperbacks, with lurid covers and titles such as *Slay-Ride for Cutie,* and *Say it with Lead*, bought furtively in a second-hand bookshop in Shrewsbury. And then there was her *Daily Telegraph*, with a few days' worth of crosswords going begging, and the two local papers that were now a tantalising blur of titbits of gossip, she had no doubt of that.

Which was precisely what she was doing at the moment, catching up on the gossip on the Number 49, getting the very latest as it stopped at each village on the way in, the passengers usually better informed than either newspaper, and without the same restraining need for accuracy.

Which is how she came to go past where she normally got off, only realising it some stops further on, listening avidly to the various candidates for the father of the new born child of somebody called Elsie Woods in Nether Myddle, unmarried, apparently, and satisfyingly brazen with it.

Clutching her handbag to her, one hand on the confection of a hat which went with the royal blue outfit she'd decided on for town, she alighted, with a flurry of goodbyes and vague apologies, in a part of Kingham she wasn't familiar with.

And it was all quite dingy, all rather down-at-heel, she considered, taking it out on the area as she resignedly walked back past a second-hand furniture shop, and a cake shop with a cat asleep in the window, and then a hairdressing salon badly in need of a lick of paint, a sign in one of its grimy windows letting her know that booking wasn't necessary.

I bet! she thought tartly.

And then the forecourt and padlocked double doors of a building with a sign on it telling her it was a motor vehicle repair shop – which didn't fool Miss Wyndham for one moment. It was perfectly clear to her that, were the police to raid it now, they'd find it piled to the rafters with stolen goods from the recent series of lorry hijacks in the Midlands. It was at times such as this that even Miss Wyndham was tempted to wonder if some of the criticism of the police wasn't indeed justified.

She came to a junction and a road she recognised then, one she knew that would take her into the town centre. She turned into it.

Just ahead of her on that side was a pub, The Royal Oak, its hanging sign said, yet another pub commemorating the escape of the future Charles 11 from Cromwellian soldiers following the Battle of Worcester.

She wondered, not for the first time, just how many public houses in the Marches were called the Royal Oak. And just how long it would have taken the young prince to get to the coast and France if he had stopped to hide in all the oak trees it was claimed he'd hidden in, and dallied in all the beds he was supposed to have dallied in, on his way there.

At least, she thought, this Royal Oak looked contemporary to that time, yellowing oak half-timbers on white-washed walls, and a porticoed entrance with a worn stone mounting block on one side.

The two men seemed suddenly to appear on the street ahead of her, and she found something instantly and unsettlingly familiar about them. They had apparently come out of one of the shops, a small row of them, just beyond the pub, and were walking in her direction.

And then she recognised them.

She came to a halt, unable to move, unable even for a moment to breathe.

They were the badger baiters, two of the badger baiters from that day. She'd spotted them several times since, or thought she had, all four of them together then, here or in Church Myddle, even coming out of the village shop once.

But now, in that instant of recognition, she was sure. Now she *knew* it was them. And she was immediately back in Cutterbach Wood, listening to their voices, excited and cruel on the summer air, watching them walking towards her.

And she shut her eyes tight again, as she had on that day, waiting for the fate she'd escaped then to catch up with her now.

And opened them again in time to see them disappearing into the pub.

Miss Wyndham stood in the middle of the pavement in her town-going royal blue outfit and matching hat, and dithered. She'd passed a phone box a few yards back. But *couldn't*, for the life of her, think at the moment whom she should tell.

And then she remembered. The police. She must tell the police, of course. The public shouldn't approach them, because they are dangerous and believed to be armed, but should contact their nearest police station or ring 999, in complete confidence.

Miss Wyndham, quivering with purpose, bustled back to the phone box, pulling the door open, muttering urgently to herself and fumbling in her handbag, in her purse, for change.

"Nine-nine-nine. Ring nine-nine-nine," she told herself, and tremblingly began dialling the Owens' number.

Annie answered.

She took down the number of the phone box, in case Miss Wyndham ran out of change, told her again not to worry, and then went to fetch Owain.

She was having none of his nonsense this time, she told him. Harriet was on the phone for him, something about the badger baiters. She sounded really upset, and if he, Owain, didn't get out of that bed this minute to speak to her, then she, Annie, would be returning with a bucket of water.

Owain, who considered that the only natural, sensible thing to do with water was to sit on it or by it, was otherwise none too fond of the stuff. He emerged, grumbling, from the depths of his bed, and reached for his trousers.

Fate, in the shape of the loss of the Hawis Stone, had lost out to the threat. Owain knew his Annie.

After Owain had talked to Miss Wyndham, and told her to stay there, in the phone box, until they arrived, he rang the Keeper's Cottage.

When there was no reply there he phoned the Hall. Shelly answered. She had no idea where Sion was but said Clem might know.

Clem was in the kitchen, at one of their regular hunt meetings with John Beecher, her fellow Joint Master. The hunt, no matter what, would still go on, its rural rhythms as deeply embedded in the lives of those who followed it as the seasons.

Sion, Clem was able to tell him, was working, doing a bit of ditching over the border at Rhanagog. And while Owain was telling her what it was about, and sounding, it struck her, a bit more like the old Owain, Humphrey walked in.

Clem asked Owain to hold on, and then quickly told him what Owain had told her.

Humphrey's meaty jaw clamped shut on the news. He was in the process of losing what, after Clem, had become most dear to him. And, like Sion, he had no doubt whom to blame for it.

Clem had to stop him haring off there and then, on his own. She decided a calmer, more responsible note was called for. She suggested to Owain that it might be best if she picked up Harriet on her own, and then reported it to the police.

Humphrey, overhearing that, was immediately against it. So was Owain, who insisted that he was going as well. And so did John Beecher, when he wandered out from the kitchen and learned what was going on. John, with his coalman's shoulders and hands a cricket ball could disappear into.

"Right! Come on, then," Clem said, having arranged to pick up Owain on the way.

She seemed to have forgotten all about striking a calmer, more responsible note, and was already on her way out of the door ahead of them.

Owain, hurriedly putting his boots on, asked Annie to ring the phone box in Kingham and tell Harriet that they were on their way.

Annie did so, and then waited, listening to it ringing on.

Chapter Thirty-Four

Miss Wyndham's nerves started to settle, now she knew that help, familiar help, was on its way. She even found she was beginning to enjoy herself.

She narrowed her eyes on the entrance of the pub, the hard-boiled private eye in *Kiss Me Deadly*, and wished she had a stick of gum to chew on. Or a cigarette. A cigarette would do. Phineas Cook's DI MacNail seemed never to be without one in his mouth, one eye half-closed against the smoke.

When a couple of people strolled past she lifted the receiver and talked into it, an ordinary member of the public making a call.

It then occurred to her that if the suspects were to do the same, were to leave the pub and walk her way, they might "make her", as she seemed to remember DI MacNail putting it.

Across the road was another small row of shops, their plate glass windows throwing back a reflection of the phone box and, more importantly, the pub.

A woman window shopping. Ideal cover.

She checked that she'd put her purse back in her handbag, and that she still had her gloves, and touched at her hat in the vanity mirror above the phone.

And then she pushed open the door, leaving the box quite casually, a professional giving nothing away, and almost walked into them as they were passing.

The one nearest to her, the younger of the two, glanced at her, and then down at her shiny, expensive-looking black leather handbag.

He made a quick sweep of the street and then lunged for it.

It was Miss Wyndham's best handbag.

She squeaked and clutched it to her.

"Give it 'ere, you old crow!" he snarled.

Miss Wyndham tightened her grip.

He was about to make another grab for it when she said in a rush, "They know who you are. They know you're the badger baiters. I've told Owain about it, told him where you are". She was no longer the cool professional but an old lady, on her own and afraid. "And DI MacNail," she remembered. "I've put him in the picture, as well. The DI knows all about it."

He frowned. "Who?"

"Detective Inspector MacNail. He's running the operation."

"What operation? Who *are* you?" he said, glancing round suspiciously.

"What does that matter? She knows who we are," the older man said. "And she's been calling somebody. Come on, Jace, let's split, before the law or whoever gets here."

"Yeah –but *how* does she know?"

"How the hell do I know? Maybe she just heard about us, or something. Maybe she's one of the badger people. I dunno. What does it matter? Come on!"

"She's been following us," it occurred to the one called Jace then.

He came up close to her and she swung her head away from the venom in his face and the smell of beer.

"Have you been following us, you old hag!" he hissed. "Have yah?"

"Yes, sure, sure, I tailed you. Then I had to go and blow my cover like some rookie!" Miss Wyndham said in her own, genteel, accent, enunciating the words carefully, a bad amateur actress, utterly miscast but doing her best.

She was dizzy with fear, disorientated, no longer sure whether what was happening was fact or fiction, whether she might not be at home, sitting up in bed, reading about it.

"You what?"Jace said with a laugh, the sound without mirth and loud in Cutterbach Wood on that quiet, early summer's morning.

"Come on, leave her," the other said to him, his eyes moving on the street. "She's trouble, whoever she is."

But something else had occurred to Jace, a sly light dawning in his eyes. "You didn't ring nobody, did you – nothing to do with us, anyhow."

"Nah, just wanted to powder my nose," Miss Wyndham said, the wisecracking Tootsie Morgan in *Until I Die.*

"She's *batty*," Jace said, grinning with recognition. "I had an old auntie like her. She ended up thinking she was Irish. Used to wander about the streets singing *Danny Boy* in her night-dress. Right," he said then to Miss Wyndham, getting back to business, "give us the bag!"

"Leave it, Jace!" his friend warned. "You don't know she didn't ring nobody. Could have a law car or something turning up any minute. Come on – let's split."

Jace hesitated. "She'll follow us. They always do that, mad people. Follow you about."

"We'll run for it. She won't be able to follow us then, will she."

"Yeah –take a powder," Miss Wyndham advised them.

"Shut up, you mad old cow," Jace snarled. "And what about if she saw us leave the flats? The pub won't tell nobody nothing, but she might have seen us come out from the flats."

"I dunno nothing, see," Miss Wyndham said, carefully, out of the corner of her mouth.

It was the older one's turn now to tell her to shut up. He was trying to think.

"Right," he said, coming to a decision, "we'll take her up to the flat, phone Mick and get him to bring the van round. Then we'll drive her about for an hour or so and dump her somewhere else. She's confused enough as it is, by that time she won't know what day it is, never mind anything else."

Miss Wyndham, who even under normal circumstances was frequently unsure what day it was, told them not to be saps.

"That's a Fed rap," she warned. Or was that transporting somebody across a state line against their will? She found she couldn't be sure.

"What," Jace said, "and show the old crow exactly where I live and how to get there? Do me a favour!"

"You could blindfold me," Miss Wyndham suggested, feeling that somehow she was both actor and spectator in this drama.

"We could kill you, you mean!" the older man growled at her. "Now you listen to me, you old bag, or it'll be the worse for you. When we start walking, you keep looking at the ground, okay? If you see where we're going, where we're taking you, we'll have to kill you, get it?"

"It will be curtains for you, sweetie," Miss Wyndham warned herself, taking her cue from *Hotsy, You'll be Chilled*.

The younger one laughed. "Be that all right, you mad old bat. We'll stick you a couple of times, and then let the dogs have a chew. Now get going."

Miss Wyndham knew how this bit went. In Phineas's latest book, *Breakfast at Mr Chow's*, gang boss Mr Chow is bundled off a Limehouse street into a car by rival gangsters, and taken to a nearby gambling den. When they leave the car, cunning Mr Chow, who's been busy tearing up a betting slip in his pocket on the way there, with his bookie's name on it and the horses it was known he was going to back that morning, surreptitiously drops the pieces across the pavement and up a passageway leading to the den.

While the two men kept an eye on the street, Miss Wyndham, their dear old auntie out for a nice little walk with them, as Jace had put it, surreptitiously felt in the pockets of her suit jacket, the cool professional again, and found torn up pieces of the betting slip waiting in both.

She dropped the first bits after they'd gone a few yards, and then marked their way up the street, turning off it into a passageway running between two of the shops in the row, to a small low-rise block of flats behind them.

The paper trail continued up the stairs to the first floor, where the last remaining pieces were dropped at the door of a flat there.

Miss Wyndham, still looking at the ground, and trying to remember how it was supposed to end, went unsteadily through it.

Chapter Thirty-Five

It was Clem who spotted the first bits of confetti on the pavement.

The phone box had been occupied when they drew up in front of it – but not by Miss Wyndham. And when the caller had finished they learnt that it had been unoccupied when he arrived there. They checked that the exchange number on the phone was the same number Miss Wyndham had given to Annie, and then tried the pub.

Owain, reading the bar at a glance when they entered, had muttered something about getting nothing in this place, which was precisely what they came away with.

They went back to the phone box and called Annie and then Shelly at the Hall. Neither of them had heard from Miss Wyndham.

Annie had suggested that, if the two men had left the pub while she was waiting in the phone box, she might have followed them. Even though told to stay there.

"You know how she's away with the fairies sometimes."

They decided to search the streets nearest to the junction first, and if there was still no sign of Miss Wyndham, one tailing two badger baiters or otherwise, then they would ring the police.

With Clem at the wheel of the shooting brake they were back at the telephone box in no time.

And it was then that she spotted the confetti.

She walked up to it.

"Confetti," she said.

"Somebody had a wedding reception in the pub," Humphrey suggested.

Owain snorted a laugh. "What – in that dump?"

"We can't all afford the Blenheim," John Beecher said, naming Kingham's swankiest hotel.

"Come on," Humphrey said impatiently, "the sooner we get the cops on to this the better."

Clem hesitated.

"What's with it?" Humphrey asked her. "Huh? What do you think the stuff is? Miss Wyndham leaving us a clue, or something?"

"I don't know. It might be," his wife said shortly, stung by his grin, and walked on, past the pub's entrance.

Humphrey looked at the other two men and shrugged.

"There's some more here," she said.

Humphrey sighed. "Yeah, well, like I say, honey, a wedding reception. Come on, let's make that call. It'll probably be better coming from you, another woman."

But Clem wasn't listening.

"Hon-ey!" Humphrey protested.

"I just want to..." she murmured vaguely, walking slowly on, searching the pavement ahead of her.

She was following her nose, following a feeling she couldn't explain, following the confetti trail that Miss Wyndham had laid for Mr Chow's gang members to follow.

The other three tagged on behind, up the street to the shops, turning into the passageway there, and up the stairs of the flats as Miss Wyndham had done, and to the door she'd gone through.

There, Humphrey dug his heels in, stopping his wife just as she was about to ring the bell.

"Hold on a minute, honey. What are you gonna say?" he said with a laugh. "Huh? Er– excuse me – say, did you by any chance kidnap a pal of ours, a little old lady called Miss Wyndham? They're probably having a wedding party in there or something. I mean –*come* on!"

"Bit quiet for a party," Owain said, whose experience of parties was largely restricted to the sort thrown on the river.

"Or maybe they've started their honeymoon early. Hon-eey!" Humphrey said, appealing to her.

Clem looked at John Beecher and then at Owain.

Owain shrugged. John looked undecided.

"Well, we've come this far," Clem said, but looking less certain now.

"Yeah. Yeah, she's right. In for a penny, in for a pound," John Beecher decided suddenly, and pressed the bell.

Inside the flat, Miss Wyndham was sitting carefully on the edge of a threadbare armchair, a figure from another world in that room, with its stained, greasy brown and orange carpet, the rose pattern on the curtains blown with grime, a Lady Bountiful in royal blue and a hat, on a mission to help the poor.

While the poor, in the persons of the two baiters, were busy helping themselves, sitting on the sofa, her jewellery and the contents of her purse on a coffee table with a peeling wood veneer top in front of them.

On a second armchair, one bare foot up on it and the tip of her tongue out in concentration, Jace's girlfriend was absorbed in painting her toenails.

She had shown a brief, mild curiosity at Miss Wyndham's appearance in the room, and had then gone back to them.

The two men were bickering over the division of Miss Wyndham's jewellery, which included her engagement ring and the signet ring of her fiancé, a young subaltern who never returned from the First World War. He had fought and died bravely, his medals, with their bright ribbons, given to her by his parents and kept in a bureau drawer, told her that story each time she took them out, heart full, to polish them.

When they had stripped those rings from her fingers it was as if she had been slapped.

It had left her feeling somehow even more alone and vulnerable, but curiously no longer confused or afraid. Just foolish and old, and mocked by a reality she only now seemed to have woken up to.

She knew now that it hadn't been a torn-up betting slip she had marked their way with, but confetti. A memory of a summer wedding she couldn't bear to empty from her suit pockets because she couldn't bear to throw it away, like rubbish.

Silly old fool, she chided herself, trying hard not to cry. Not here. Not in front of them. No matter what they did to her.

Because she also remembered, also knew now, how it had ended for Mr Chow. And knew that it wouldn't end that way for her.

In Breakfast at Mr Chow's, the members of his gang searching for him spotted the trail he'd left and burst through the door of the den, just as their boss was about to be dispatched to his ancestors.

But this was real life, not fiction. And real life rarely comes bursting through the door at the last minute, Miss Wyndham told herself bravely, just as the doorbell went.

"That'll be Mick," Jace said.

Chapter Thirty-Six

The door of the flat opened, and Humphrey, about to get in first and apologise for bothering them, frowned.

He'd seen that face before somewhere.

Jace, taking in Humphrey and his shirt, didn't need to think where he'd seen him before.

And then Humphrey got it. Cutterbach Wood. He was the baiter in the hole. The one who'd tried to give him a crew cut with a spade.

Then, his bare chest sleek with sweat and mud, he had slipped from Humphrey's grasp like a bar of soap. Now, given a second go, Humphrey took it. One hand like a baseball mitt shot out and stopped the door about to be slammed on them, while the other grabbed Jace by the arm.

"*Gotcha!*"

Humphrey didn't bother doing any more thinking after that.

Telling the others over his shoulder that this was one of the baiters, he almost ran Jace ahead of him down the hall and through the first, open door he came to.

Miss Wyndham saw the baiter reappear, followed by what appeared to be Batch Magna trooping in, led by Sir Humph, and told herself that it was all right, she was just having another funny turn, that's all.

"And that guy's another one!" Humphrey grinned in recognition and stabbed a finger as the other baiter stood up. "It's the one Sion slugged. You can tell by his nose," he said, and then blinked, his grin widening with surprised delight as he took in Miss Wyndham.

The older and bigger of the two men looked ready to run, or fight. Until John Beecher stepped forward.

"Sit down," he advised him quietly.

The baiter looked at him, weighing up his shoulders and that steady calmness, and sat down.

Miss Wyndham, who'd gone from not believing it, not daring to believe it, and then allowing herself to believe it, got dazedly to her feet and walked into a hug from Clem.

Humphrey dumped Jace on the sofa with the other man, watched by his girlfriend, showing a little more interest in things now, taking in his shirt and baseball cap with a look of anticipation, as if waiting for the entertainment to start.

Owain looked at the handbag and the other things on the coffee table.

"Is this your stuff, Hattie?" he asked.

"Yes, yes, it is, Owain. And they took my rings," she said. Meaning the engagement and signet rings, meaning they took much more than that, much more than her purse and the other jewellery.

"And just what were you gonna do with the lady, huh?" Humphrey asked, looming over them.

"They were gonna take me for a ride," Miss Wyndham said, remembering her lines, prompted by Humphrey's Bronx accent. "The one-way kind."

"No, we bloody wasn't!" the older baiter said, rising in alarm, until pushed back by Humphrey.

"Language!" Owain growled.

"We weren't going to do anything like that. Just drive her round a bit, that's all. Get her a bit more confused, like. You can't pin nothing else on us!"

"What do you mean, a bit *more* confused?" Owain said loyally. "You want to watch who you're bloody well talking about, boy! Who else is here, in the flat?" he wanted to know then.

"And what about the dogs, they here?" Humphrey put in, remembering the remark made in Cutterbach about can-opener teeth.

Jace said there was nobody else there, and while John Beecher took a look in the kitchen off the room, Owain went to see for himself.

John reappeared a few minutes later, waving an empty gallon can.

"They can add criminal damage to robbery and kidnapping old ladies. DDT. There's more cans in there, shoved under the sink. No question now who poisoned the birds."

Humphrey lifted bunched fists and shook them in the air in front of the two men, his meaty features clenched. They shrunk back on the sofa and waited for him to fall on them, but it was out of frustration at what he'd liked to do to them, rather than what he intended to.

John went off to see what Owain was up to, and Clem got Miss Wyndham, still dazed-looking, but in a perfectly happy sort of way, to sit down again, before looking round for a phone and spotting one on top of a television.

She glanced at Jace's girlfriend on her way across to it, and did a double take.

Feeling perhaps that she should take a more active part in things, she was carefully putting the top back on her nail varnish. She flinched when Clem suddenly leant down to look at the single pendant stone she was wearing around her neck, before lifting the chain over her head.

"Hey!" she protested.

"Shut up," Clem told her absently, gazing at the stone, at the intense flame burning in it the colour of a blood orange, the ancient heat of a fire opal, on a Welsh gold mount and chain.

She turned it over, to the date and motto engraved on the back of the mount: *Beati Qui Durant 1661*

"It is ..." she said wonderingly.

"Humphrey," she said in a still voice.

Humphrey was busy addressing the two on the sofa, getting a few things off his chest about suffering birds and cowards who sneak in at night with their poison – a woman's weapon, he was able to add sneeringly, remembering Miss Wyndham telling him about typical poisoners, and seeing that they weren't doctors.

It was her use of his full name that caught his attention. His wife usually shortened it to Humph, but in serious or tender moments it was always Humphrey.

"Humphrey," she said, holding the pendant up by its chain. "Recognise this?"

Humphrey frowned at it.

"It's the Hawis Stone," she said.

"It's the *Hawis Stone*," she said again, as if it were only now beginning to sink in, and laughed delightedly at the sheer luck of the thing.

"*Jeeze...*" he breathed. "Jeeze, it is, too! Where – ?"

"She had it. She was wearing it. She's even had the clasp repaired, look," Clem said, handing it to Humphrey, handing him back four hundred years of his family's history.

"Yes, I did – I had it fixed. It's mine," the girl said, as if that settled it.

"No, it's not, dear," Clem said patiently. "It's stolen property. And you're in possession of it. But don't worry, the police will explain it to you."

The girl digested that. "I ain't done nothing! It was him," she said then, pointing at Jace. "He nicked it. It was in a handbag he snatched."

"You bitch!"Jace snarled at her, and scrambling over the back of the sofa made a run for the door, to be fielded by John Beecher, walking back into the room with Owain.

"Where you off to then?" he said casually, and turning him around gave him a start back to the sofa. "Well, there's nobody else here. Nor no dogs."

"And the state of the place, man!" Owain said. "Makes our Sion look house proud, it does. And it was them, I hear, that was throwing DDT about. Not that it will do any good now. Too late for that," he added, Welsh gloom coming in again like weather.

And then Humphrey held up the pendant.

Only Miss Wyndham, when she was shown it, shown what she, with her paper trail, had led them to, looked unsurprised at its reappearance. But by then it would have taken a great deal more than that to surprise Miss Wyndham.

"I've no hope of getting my handbag and the rest of the things back, I don't suppose," Clem said. "But that doesn't matter, now we have this. And we've got Harriet to thank for it."

"And you to thank, Clem, for finding Harriet," John Beecher pointed out. "If it had been left to us …"

"The confetti, apparently, was from her suit pockets – it was left over from our wedding," she told Humphrey.

"Yeah, well, I guess I owe you an apology, honey," Humphrey said sheepishly.

"Yes. I guess you do, darling," Clem said, and smiled sweetly at him.

Jace's girlfriend fell over herself to tell her, when Clem, picking up the phone, asked for the flat number and the rest of the address.

"Well, I'm glad it's back again in the family, and all that, course I am," Owain said glumly. "But it don't change nothing, does it? I mean, it won't bring the shoot back, or the fishing, will it? And what did they put in the river?" it occurred to him then. "That's what I'd like to bloody well know."

"Nothing – we ain't been near your poxy river!" the older baiter snarled when he put it to them.

Owain looked at him with an expression John Beecher had seen before.

"Owain," he said, touching his arm. "Owain, let the police deal with it."

"You want to watch your bloody manners, boy," Owain said, reluctantly leaving it at that.

Clem put the phone down. "They're sending someone."

She went and sat on the arm of Miss Wyndham's chair. "The police are on their way, Hattie. You'll soon be home with the kettle on."

"Look at these bloody curtains," Owain said, tutting on Annie's behalf at the state of them.

Not more than five minutes later, the doorbell rang again, breaking the waiting silence in the room.

"That was quick," John Beecher said.

"That'll be Mick," Miss Wyndham blurted out. "I remember now. They phoned someone called Mick. Told him to bring the van round, because they had something they wanted dumped. Meaning me, I suppose," she added, looking indignantly at the two on the sofa.

"Could be a couple more of the lads with him, as well. And maybe the dogs. This could get interesting," the elder baiter smirked, looking at Owain.

"Well, better let whoever in then, eh, Owain?" John Beecher said easily, and disappeared into the hall, reappearing a few moments later followed by a man Humphrey recognised immediately as the one he had walloped with the axe shaft, and two uniformed police officers.

"We know he belongs here," the older one, a sergeant, said, looking round the crowded room, his eyes pausing on Humphrey's shirt and baseball cap. "We're old friends, aren't we, Michael. Though you wouldn't think it, the way he tried to skedaddle when he saw us. But he's got a bad leg. What happened, Michael, fall off a drainpipe? Ah, and there's our Danny and

Jason there," he added, nodding at the two on the sofa. "Well, this *is* cosy."

"We weren't sure who was at the door," Clem said. "We didn't expect you to be here quite so soon."

"We were in the area when we got the call. And you are, Madam?"

Clem told him, and was about to introduce the others, when the sergeant put up a hand as if stopping the traffic.

"Hold on, please," he said, and taking his time over it, removed a notebook and Biro from a top pocket.

"Humph," Humphrey said amiably, when it was his turn to give his name. "Strange," he added on a more sober note, seeing the Sergeant's expression.

"Humphrey. *Sir* Humphrey Strange," Miss Wyndham, a stickler for such things, put in.

"Yeah," Humphrey said, and gave a small embarrassed laugh when the Sergeant's eyebrows went up.

"And *Lady* Clementine Strange," Miss Wyndham added, filling in the bits Clem had left out.

The Sergeant looked unimpressed.

"So what's all this about then?" he asked, his tone suggesting that, whatever it was about, he knew he wasn't going to like it.

They hadn't gone into details on the car radio, but whatever it was about, with just under an hour to go before his shift was due to finish, he could have done without it. Because whatever the story was here, with three local tearaways and a couple of aristocrats in it, one an American in a shirt, he just knew that it was not going to be a straightforward one.

He looked up from his notebook, and then looked where everyone else was looking – at Miss Wyndham, who shifted nervously on her chair.

"Well, it all began, officer," she said then, confidingly, leaning towards him over the handbag clutched on her lap, "on the Number Forty-Nine bus from Batch Magna. Or though," she reconsidered, frowning conscientiously, "to be strictly truthful about it, it was really Elsie Woods from Nether Myddle who started it. Not that one listens to common gossip, of course, but she's unmarried, you know, and …"

Chapter Thirty-Seven

Over the following few weeks it was Miss Wyndham who was the talk of the Number 49 bus and the centre of rapt attention on her frequent journeys on it to Kingham– far more frequent than was strictly necessary, if the truth be known.

And it was Miss Wyndham whose picture now looked out from the front pages of the two weekly local newspapers she took, in the royal blue outfit and hat. She was on the front page of the other locals as well, the papers she bought furtively in Kingham, hurrying back with them stuffed in a shopping bag to add to the rest of her press cuttings, as she believed they were called.

She was even interviewed on Border Radio, introduced by a nice young lady who described her as the heroine in royal blue. She *even* received quite a few letters congratulating her on her presence of mind, and a couple admiring her outfit and wanting to know where she'd bought it.

Her fan mail, as she thought of them, before almost immediately losing patience with herself. She was behaving, she told her cats, like some silly film actress, and it had to stop.

But not before, as chief prosecution witness at the robbery and abduction trial, she paused brazenly on the steps of the court for more press attention, dressed again in what, in a defiant, unblushing moment, she thought of as her trademark royal blue suit. And not before a repeat performance – although to a disappointingly much smaller press audience – as, again, chief prosecution witness at a second trial, when the fourth baiter, the dog man, joined the other three in the dock on a joint charge of trespass and attempted badger baiting.

But when she found herself considering a rack of dark glasses in the chemist's, she decided that enough really was enough.

She had the suit cleaned, and when it came back she put it away again, firmly, in the wardrobe.

But the real, abiding, story to come out of Miss Wyndham's Kingham adventure was told just a few days after the recovery of the Hawis Stone. It turned up at Batch Hall in the person of Mr Pryce-Walker, the new owner of Home Farm, which Humphrey on inheriting had been obliged to sell to meet death duties.

It was Mr Pryce-Walker who had donated the use of Taddle-brook Leasow for the wedding celebrations, and who with his wife had been a guest at the Hall countless times, both at the late squire's table, and then that of the new American model, as he'd cheerfully described Humphrey, and his young wife, the delightful Clem.

But Mr Pryce-Walker was afraid that this time his visit was not a social one.

He had, he declared, standing in the hall with them, looking embarrassed but determined, brown trilby in hand, a confession to make.

He had, as they knew, two other farms in the valley, and while he wasn't offering it as an excuse, it did make it difficult to keep an eye on every nut and bolt. That, as he'd pointed out rather forcibly earlier today to the manager of Home Farm, was what he employed a manager to do.

Nevertheless, Mr Pryce-Walker qualified, it had happened on his property and he must therefore take full responsibility for it. Which was what had obliged him to visit them in person.

Clem and Humphrey waited. Mr Pryce-Walker cleared his throat.

He was aware, of course, he went on, of their current difficulties and was afraid that when it came to the polluting of the river and the consequences of it, he, however indirectly, must hold himself to be the cause. His manager at Home Farm had, that morning, reported a leak in a slurry tank on one of the fields near the Cluny.

The contents, for god knows how long, had been steadily leaking into a drainage ditch and from there down into the river.

As he said, he admitted full responsibility and due reparation would be made. His solicitors would be in touch to suggest appropriate recompense.

As they also knew, he had spent many an hour on the water with Owain Owen, and so had some idea what was involved in terms of the loss of fishing revenue and the cost of restocking, plus the distress the incident had caused. All that, he could assure them, would be taken into account. And then, perhaps, they could, if necessary, take the business on from there, when some sort of figure had been arrived at.

Mr Pryce-Walker then added, a little more informally, having got all that off his chest, that he was most *frightfully* sorry.

Humphrey wanted to give him a shoulder hug, he looked so damn stiff-upper-lip British and embarrassed, but had been in the country long enough to know that you do not hug gentleman farmers in hairy tweed suits.

Clem, glancing at her husband, knew what that expression meant. Humphrey, with the sale of the Hall almost completed, and money then to spare, was about to tell Mr Pryce-Walker to *for-get* it, to wave away with that generous hand of his all that damn boring stuff about compensation and lawyers – heck, he didn't spring the leak himself, did he!

Clem got there first. She thanked Mr Pryce-Walker for his visit, and asked if he would take tea, and Mr Pryce-Walker thanked Clem, and said that he'd be delighted. And then moving into the kitchen started discussing the weather.

And Humphrey, not for the first time since arriving there, thought that there were those in this country, himself included, who spoke English and those who spoke even more English. A language which he, Humphrey, no matter how long he lived here, knew he would never fully understand.

Chapter Thirty-Eight

When the letter from Mr Pryce-Walker's solicitors arrived at the end of that week it was awhile before it was realised just what exactly it meant.

"Jeez!" was all Humphrey said, his mouth open at the suggested figure quoted in it.

And then Clem sat down, slowly, with the letter at the kitchen table, muttering to herself and jotting down calculations on the back of the envelope.

She added the figures up, and stared at the result.

She went over them again, carefully, even inflating some of them, to be on the safe side, and the total still told her the same thing.

She looked up at Humphrey.

"Humph. Humphrey, do you know what this means?" she said, not sounding as if she did herself entirely.

"What?" Humphrey said, frowning. "Hey, we're not going to argue with it, are we? I mean, it's –"

Clem put up a hand, shutting him up, and checked them again, wondering if she had left anything out. She decided she hadn't.

"Well – well, as far as I can see," she said, laughing, "this means that, if we're careful, we don't have to go!"

"What?" Humphrey said, after deciding that no, he wasn't sure he did understand her.

"We can stay on," she told him simply.

Humphrey thought about it again.

"What?" he said then. "Stay on, stay on, d'you mean? Here? At the Hall?"

"Yes. Stay on. Here. At the Hall. Humphrey, we can *stay*," she said, as if fully realising it herself now, and, pushing her chair back, flung herself at him.

"So we don't have to sell?" Humphrey said, disentangling himself, wanting to make sure he had it straight.

"No, darling, we don't have to sell."

"Jeez!" he said for the second time that morning.

Clem sat down again with her figures. "It will be tight, but we're used to that. We'll have enough to restock the coverts and the river, to pay rates and services, and enough to live on until they start producing income. We can do it *–just*. But we can do it. Humphrey – Humph, we can *do* it!"

It was Humphrey's turn to sit down.

She looked at him, her eyes bright.

"It was the Hawis Stone that gave it to us. Its loss took it away, as it was said it would, and the finding of it gave it back again."

Humphrey said nothing. In some unreformed part of him he still thought it was all a load of horse feathers. He still, where no one could hear him say it, called it coincidence. But just in case, and because you never know, he stayed silent.

He shook his head instead. "Jeez – I cannot be*lieve* it."

"Yes, I know," Clem laughed. "I *know!*"

"Wait till Owain hears! And Sion! They're not gonna believe it, neither."

"I'll ring round in a minute and tell everyone."

"And we'll have a jolly," Humphrey said.

"Oh, *yes*, we must!"

"We'll have the biggest jolly since – since –"

"Since the last jolly," Clem said.

"Since the last jolly," he said, laughing with her. "We'll invite everybody. *Every*body."

"Especially Miss Wyndham."

"Especially Miss Wyndham."

"And Mr and Mrs Pryce-Walker."

"Yeah, and Mr and Mrs Pryce-Walker," Humphrey said happily, glancing round the kitchen, the place where their parties always seemed to end up.

But seeing far more than the kitchen in that glance. Seeing the entire house there, seeing the stairs being run up on, and the banisters being slid down on, and pillow fights at bedtime, and trees being climbed and dens made and ball games and picnics and fishing and messing about in boats – seeing them everywhere, like ferrets. Seeing what he had seen many times, seeing their future there.

And it came home fully to him then, all that staying on really meant.

"Yeah …" he said, his grin widening. "*Yeah!*"

And not only that …

A couple of days after the party, Clem returned in the morning from a trip to Church Myddle.

Humphrey was up a stepladder in an upstairs corridor, busy with a paint roller and their plans to open the Hall to the public, breaking vigorously now and then into songs he almost immediately forgot the words to, short bursts of a happiness that had to go somewhere, escaping from him like steam.

Clem suggested he take a break, and join her in the kitchen for tea and biscuits.

While standing by the electric kettle, waiting for it to boil, she said, as if just remembering it, that she had something to tell him.

"Oh, yeah?" he said absently.

He was sitting at the table, idly glancing through the copy of the *Church Myddle Chronicle* Clem had brought in with her, its pages bare now of Miss Wyndham in royal blue.

"Humph, I'm preggers," she said lightly, flippantly even.

He looked up blankly.

"Pregnant," she translated.

He was unsure how he was supposed to take it, seeing that she'd called him Humph, and the way she'd said it. It was difficult to tell sometimes, with Clem's sort of English English.

"What?" he asked, frowning and alert.

"I'm pregnant," she said in an airy sort of way.

He cocked his head. "What, pregnant, pregnant?" he said carefully, and tapped his ample front a few times as if using sign language, but wanting to get this, of all things, absolutely straight.

"Yes," she said, laughing. "That pregnant. Having a baby pregnant. Nearly two months' pregnant pregnant. According to the doctor. Humph– we're going to have a baby!"

Humphrey looked shocked.

"We're going to have a baby," he told himself. "We're having a baby!" he said, shooting to his feet as if ready for some sort of action.

"We're having a baby!" he told her.

"But not quite yet, darling," she said, laughing again, as he hugged her gingerly.

He stepped back to get a good look at her, tried to say what he couldn't find the words for, kissed her instead, took another look at her, and then did it all again, before taking off round the kitchen, grinning at her and shaking his head – as if to say he had to hand it to her, he *had* to hand it to her.

He sat down, jumped up again and insisted that *she* sit down, and when she protested that the kettle had boiled, said he'd make the tea, and immediately went for another spin round the kitchen.

And then he stopped and looked at her.

"Anything else? I mean, first the Hall and now a baby. You got anything else?" he asked, as if in appeal.

Clem laughed. "No, darling, that's all for now."

He took off again round the kitchen, glancing at her every few paces or so, as if in suspicion, as if still not entirely convinced, as if he wouldn't put it past her – he would *not* put it past her.

A man who had never known such happiness, and one who wasn't at all sure at that moment if he could take any more.

But he would have to – because not only *that* …

Follow the continuing Batch Magna story in *The Batch Magna Caper*

221

Preview

In another memorable tale in the Batch Magna Chronicles, a hapless gang of crooks, led by self-styled criminal mastermind pawnbroker Harold Sneed, pull off 'the big one', a wages snatch at a factory in Shrewsbury. Two gang members take the money from there by train back to Birmingham, changing at a station almost on the doorstep of Sir Humphrey of Batch Hall.

It's there that things start to unravel. The money goes missing. Misunderstanding follows misunderstanding, until it leads them to Batch Hall when everyone is busy with a historical re-enactment show. Among the replica firearms is a real gun, carried by Harold Sneed with murderous intent and Humphrey in mind.

Sneed is now convinced that Humphrey – an overweight former short-order cook from the Bronx – is a Mafia mobster laying low. And on top of this, he believes Humph has his money; as a result, the spectators for the re-enactment find that there's an extra event on the programme.

The Batch Magna Chronicles, Volume Three

COMING SOON

About the Author

Peter Maughan's early ambition to be a landscape painter ran into a lack of talent – or enough of it to paint to his satisfaction what he saw. He worked on building sites, in wholesale markets, on fairground rides and in a circus. And travelled the West Country, roaming with the freedom of youth, picking fruit, and whatever other work he could get, sleeping wherever he could, before moving on to wherever the next road took him. A journeying out of which came his non-fiction work *Under the Apple Boughs*, when he came to see that he had met on his wanderings the last of a village England. After travelling to Jersey in the Channel Islands to pick potatoes, he found work afterwards in a film studio in its capital, walk-ons and bit parts in the pilot films that were made there, and as a contributing scriptwriter. He studied at the Actor's Workshop in London, and worked as an actor in the UK and Ireland (in the heyday of Ardmore Studios). He founded and ran a fringe theatre in Barnes, London and, living on a converted Thames sailing barge among a small colony of houseboats on the River Medway, wrote pilot film scripts as a freelance deep in the green shades of rural Kent. An idyllic, heedless time in that other world of the river, which later, when he had collected enough rejection letters learning his craft as a novelist, he transported to a river valley in the Welsh Marches, and turned into the Batch Magna novels. Peter is married and lives currently in Wales. Visit his website at www.batchmagna.com.

Note from the Publisher

If you enjoyed this book, we are delighted to share also *The Famous Cricket Match*, a short story by Peter Maughan, featuring our hero Sir Humphrey of Batch Hall, defending the village with both cricket *and* baseball…

To get your **free copy of *The Famous Cricket Match***, as well as receive updates on further releases in the Batch Magna Chronicles series, sign up at http://farragobooks.com/batch-magna-signup